Angels Only Stand Where Cherubim Take Flight

by Victoria Ellison

PublishAmerica
Baltimore

© 2005 by Victoria Ellison.
All rights reserved. No part of this book may be reproduced, stored in a retrieval system or transmitted in any form or by any means without the prior written permission of the publishers, except by a reviewer who may quote brief passages in a review to be printed in a newspaper, magazine or journal.

First printing

ISBN: 1-4137-9477-7
PUBLISHED BY PUBLISHAMERICA, LLLP
www.publishamerica.com
Baltimore

Printed in the United States of America

To Daddy

Photos by Frank Zingale.

Special thanks to
Anne Creager
Len Munks
Willie Pace
and Raymond Basie.

When people ask me why I am a social worker, I laugh and answer, "Well, it certainly is not for the money," which is a private joke that I keep to myself. No, I certainly don't do it for the money. If you had asked me when I was young, I'd simply tell you I just want to help people, young boys in particular who found themselves in the juvenile justice system. But the real reason I stay is... way beyond what any ordinary individual would understand. This is a story. A story about how my worst nightmare helped me find my oasis, like one someone would find to help him survive through the desert.

Chapter 1

My name is Jeremiah Washington. I came into this world the year before JFK was assassinated. Born to Anthony and Georgia Washington, a full eight pounds and three ounces, at exactly at 11:59 on October 31, 1962. Any later than that and I would have been born the day after Halloween. I was born with six fingers on both hands. Estelle White, my grandmother saw this as a sign from the heavens and informed my mother I was going to be special. Mama named me Jeremiah after the prophet in the Bible, saying I would be close to God. My father died when I was five; he had overdosed on some drugs. At that time I didn't know what "overdosed" meant, but I remember overhearing Mama tell Grandma they found an empty bottle of sleeping pills in the trash in a motel where they found his body. I don't remember too much about him, though at the funeral, I remember asking my mother if he was really my father. When she told me yes I had a hard time believing her, because he never was around, and what I do remember I wanted badly to forget. He was a drug addict and he beat my mama.

The funeral itself was an experience. There was a lady there. Mama was yelling at her.

"You won't get a dime of my husband's insurance money," she said. "I don't care whose children you claim you had."

My Grandmother took us outside the church, explaining to my sister and me, "We'll just sit out here while your mama and the young lady talk this thing out."

My mother was my grandmother's only living child. That young woman at the funeral I discovered, was my father's other woman.

After we buried my father, we moved in with my grandmother. We didn't have a whole lot, I remember packing up after Mama had sold everything, even my bicycle that had the training wheels still on it. I cried when my mother explained to me that we could only take what could fit in the car. Soon our Chicago home was empty. Mama put us in the car and we were on our way to Cleveland.

Even though I was sad to be leaving my friends, I was glad to be moving with my Grandmother, her house had warmth to it, unlike the old house we were moving from. The sink in the kitchen always have a red, faded checkered dishcloth folded neatly across the dripping faucet. The kitchen always smelled of bleach, as if she had just been cleaning, and she would always be in the process of baking something, cakes, cookies, fudge or some type of pie. I sat in the back seat and watched out the back window till the houses on our street disappeared. I thought of the warm reception which awaited us in Cleveland. I watched as the entire neighborhood disappeared, then I sat down in the seat and played with my matchbox car, one of my few remaining toys.

My grandmother would be glad to see us. Me, Mama, and my sister April, who I occasionally called Miss Polly Purebred after the cartoon character in Underdog, we lived on Way Street off of Ninety-third, and Mama took a job at a dry cleaner across town. I started school; I don't remember too much about that except I failed kindergarten. I couldn't read, and my comprehension was poor. My sister used to tease me, in fact the whole neighborhood teased me.

"You failed the kindergarten," they'd chant daily, behind my back, on the way home, and also at recess.

I liked living with my grandmother, but I missed my old home. I even blamed my mother for my failure, saying to my friends, that if I were in Chicago I wouldn't have failed. I explained that the schools are better in Chicago. I was also having nightmares. I dreamt that my dad came back. I remember I used to hear my mother cry at night. But I wouldn't say anything because I knew she was hurting.

There was a heater that ran up from the basement and before it stopped in my room it connected to the kitchen right underneath the kitchen table. At night, I'd listen through the vent in my room and overhear Mama and Grandma talking. Mama would tell stories about my father. And about how intelligent April and I would turn out to be. Mama would often share with Grandma her dreams for us to go to college.

ANGELS ONLY STAND
WHERE CHERUBIM TAKE FLIGHT

One day when I was in the third grade, my teacher had us read out loud in class. She had us all take turns row by row. I was in the second row; fourth in line. My chair was toward the back of the classroom. When it came my turn to read, my throat tightened and I was nervous.

I read the first word "Whaat." The class broke out in laughter the teacher hushed them. I swallowed and continued "mayke thee the…."

I tried, but I could not read the words, nor sound them out. My classmates began to snicker and laugh. This made me all the more nervous. My throat tightened once more.

"Ice," Miss Hunter said trying to help me along.

I repeated "ice."

I studied the next word "Aah… mmmeeelt."

She rescued me by saying, "Okay, let's go onto the next person," saving me from any further embarrassment. But that's when it hit me, I couldn't read and what made matters worse is what happened later. A couple days after that, Mama came home one night, crying, telling Grandma how she had gone to a parent/teacher conference and my teachers said that I was learning disabled, I had poor reading and math skills and that I would need to go into special classes in order for me to pass successfully to the next grade. She also told Mama to get me tested, recommending that when I got into junior high, to place me into special classes. I would have to learn a trade because I would probably never go to college. I cried as I listened, tears flowing down my cheeks, ashamed, thinking to myself that this confirmed my beliefs about myself. It was true. I was either stupid or worse, retarded.

I think after that night I became determined. I was going to prove to the world that I was neither stupid nor retarded. I began to get books from the library, and take them home to my grandma, who I made read for me until I learned the words myself. I would even ask the teacher for an old set of flash cards so that my grandmother could quiz me at home. I knew my grandmother suspected something, but she just encouraged me to do my best.

One day she asked me, "What is this new interest in reading and in math?"

"I want to be smart, Grandma," I told her.

She patted me on my shoulder and smiled as she said, "Jeremiah, that is an honorable thing to desire."

However, I'd continued to stay up listening to their conversations at night and whenever Mama would excuse herself, I'd hurry and pull the covers over my face, close my eyes, and pretend to be asleep, because she always would check on me and my sister before she went to bed. When morning came, I quickly learned how to hide my emotions; I couldn't let Grandma see that I was listening to their adult conversations. Things that were forbidden for children to hear. I would say my tender goodbyes and slither away to school sleepy, and full of anger, many times because of what I heard the previous night.

My childhood friends were Robert Elliot, nicknamed Rob, and James Campbell, whom we called J.C. for short. I met them in kindergarten; they lived in the same neighborhood as I did and we were inseparable like the three musketeers, only not quite as famous. We just about did everything together; when we were in elementary we took the school bus home together since we lived within two blocks of each other. After we would get off the bus, the arguments were settled, and we'd always chase the girls home, playing tag with them. However, my friends would leave me behind to go to junior high and then onto high school.

Rob was a basketball player in junior high. He was the high school coach's dream, even the private schools wanted him. Even though his father was dead, it was his father's dying wish that his son would go to college, but he could go from high school straight through to the NBA. He was the truly NBA hopeful for the eighties.

J.C. on the other hand was girl crazy. I often wondered if he took something to make him like girls so much. He was the only person I knew that could date girls that were all friends, at the same time, and have them all thinking he liked each one better than he liked all the others. Then on top of that, he got Francis, this girl that really liked him and hung around him most of the time, to beat up any girl who did or said anything he didn't like. Besides being silly and immature, he was truly a genius in his own mind.

I had a separate agenda. I liked girls. A lot of them seemed to be attracted to me although didn't date a lot of them. I became friends with most girls before I actually dated them. I wasn't athletic, but I was smart. My frenzy had paid off; I could now read at the ninth grade level, but it was the comprehension I had a hard time with. My teacher Mrs. Marcs called me a late bloomer; she noticed I was doing much better than I had done in elementary. She was so impressed, she would help me after school with my reading and comprehension. She often would tell me maybe when I got to high school I could probably go into regular classes. She said I had the drive and the determination to succeed. I was motivated and anxious about learning more than anyone else in my class and I still was trying to prove to the world I wasn't retarded and I could go to college like anyone else. I wanted to go to college but I wasn't sure for what. Mrs. Marcs said that was okay, I would discover something when I got older, I was still young and discovering my world.

During my first couple years at junior high, we hung out together. Rob and J.C. and I would go to the weekend dances. But it wasn't Rob or me that would get into trouble. While we were at a dance at a Catholic School one night, J.C. was with one of his girlfriends named Tennie, short for Towanda, that he meet at a basketball game at Benedictine. They had a good team but they were no match for the "master," the nickname they gave Rob. He played along with Terrence, Maurice and another boy they called Holiday. They helped made up our basketball team one of the best in Cleveland. Anyway, we were at this dance and J.C. is talking to this girl and guess who walks up on him... Francis. She was cussing and screaming, ready to fight him and Tennie both. It took me and Rob to get her off J.C.

He kept repeating, "Girl, what's wrong with you?" as she punched him in his head. We laughed as we saw him chase Francis down the street, trying to explain why he was with that girl.

Tennie couldn't believe what she just saw. She asked Rob and me who Francis was. Remaining loyal to J.C., we lied, explaining to Tennie that our friend just broke up with the young lady, and she couldn't take the heat. One of the adult escorts politely told our party that we would have to leave the premises, no fighting was allowed on the school grounds. We reminded the older gentleman that we weren't the ones fighting, matter of fact we were the ones that tried to break it up. He told us since the young man was with our party we had to leave with him. Well J.C. was nowhere in sight, so Rob and I got into the car and asked Tennie if she would like a ride home. She said "yes" so Rob drove her home, making sure she would get there safely.

I started dating when I was well into my last year at junior high. I remember the first girl I dated, her name was Toni. We were actually good friends in junior high. I took her to the movies, well actually we double dated with Rob and his date. It was Rob who showed me how to put my arm around Toni and he knew because his cousin showed him. Then after I placed my arm around her, I kissed her. I remember Rob's cousin Theodore would show us Playboy magazines. He was a lot older that Rob, J.C. and I, and it was at a time that I'll always remember, because Toni was the first girl I had sex with. I would go over to her house; her mother was always at work in the evening.

One day I asked her if she wanted to go all the way. She did and we did. We went out together a lot. At least until her mother caught me over at her house in the bedroom naked. She then had to go over to her aunt's house after school. That put a strain on our relationship; we could only see each other at school. Then her mother decided to move to Toledo, but by that time we were not seeing each other. She'd started dating someone else and I was taken out of the picture, just like her mother and my mother hoped. I remember when my mother found out I was sexually active, I was placed on punishment. I could not leave the house for two months and no telephone and I didn't come off punishment until May. That's how her mother and my mother had succeeded in breaking us up before the school year was over.

June came, and my graduation from junior high school was coming up in a couple of weeks. My grandmother stopped me before I ran out the door for school.

"Jeremiah, I need to speak to you," she said. She was sweating, and had a stern look on her face. A dishcloth was in her hand and she smelled like bleach. She had been cleaning in the kitchen. I immediately wondered what she wanted.

"Who are you taking to the school dance?" she asked.

I explained, "I am not going to the dance at school, Grandma." I informed her that someone I knew in school was having a party in his back yard up the street and I would be going there.

"Are you taking one of your female friends?" she asked.

"I haven't asked anyone yet. Why?"

"Well, there's Carla, she lives up the street. Why don't you take her? You two used to play together when you were younger," she said. "She's a nice girl, good parents, and she goes to church every Sunday." Blah, blah, blah.

After "Sunday," I kind of tuned her out. So I was forced to listen to what was first a simple request that turned into a speech about church girls versus the girls of the world. By the time my grandmother finished talking to me I was late for school, and convinced that what I needed to do was to start dating girls that went to church. That's how she met her husband when she was young and by the time she finished high school she was married.

So I ended up taking Carla Jones to the graduation party that year, being held up the street that night. She was a quiet girl, never said much, and a beautiful creation of God. When we arrived at the party, it was in full throttle. I left Carla for a moment while I went to talk to my friends, then I came back and started talking to her. Carla, on the other hand, didn't seem to be enjoying herself, so I decided to try and cheer her up.

"There's beer here. Would you like a beer?"

"No," she said bluntly, "I don't drink." I thought to myself, *She's really not enjoying herself at this party*.

"You want to go to the park?"

"No," she answered. *Well*, I thought to myself, *that means you're not getting none tonight*.

"Actually, I'm ready to go home," she said.

The speech about church girls and girls of the world immediately came to mind as I was reminded by the tone in her voice that she was a church girl and I was a young man of the world. Anyhow, to sum things up, I blew it. *Offering her beer, what's wrong with you?* I thought. I admit I had one thing on my mind. After I admitted to myself the date was over, I took her hand and guided her through the crowd. We made it to the sidewalk and began to walk up the street.

"What time is it?" she asked.

"'Bout 10:30," I answered looking at my watch.

After that we walked in dead silence, with my mouth shut tight and head looking down staring at my shoes. As I walked, all I could do is think about how we played together as children, but after elementary school we grew apart, now it seemed like we lived in two separate worlds, and her world seem to be a bit better than mine. I looked up when we arrived at her house.

"Well, I'll see you later," she said.

"Bye," I said, but I didn't leave then. I watched her enter the house. The lights on the front porch were still on. I have to admit I was a little angry with my grandmother, I just felt that when she got married things were a lot different. People were a lot different, besides it was a long time ago, and she lived on a farm anyway. Girls are different now, the girls these days don't want to get married right out of high school, they're more independent, and want to go to college and have careers. I'd seen too many women on TV burning bras and preaching about "women's lib." Maybe Carla was like them, I didn't know. It's confusing, dating. Even for someone as young as I was at that time. You don't know whether to kiss or shake their hand goodbye. I just gave Carla the benefit of the doubt, I did neither. I just waited till she was inside the house. She didn't even turn around to acknowledge to me she was entering the house, or to even say thanks for walking her home. She just meandered inside the house. I saw her father standing in the doorway waving to me as if to say "thanks" and then once they were inside, the porch lights went out. I walked away thinking, *At least he appreciated my manners.* I looked at my watch. Since it was still early I headed back to the party. As I walked further down the street, I noticed my sister and her friends standing around the front porch of my house. I think they had just come back from the mall.

"What's wrong? Your girlfriend not enjoying the party?" my sister shouted. Ignoring her I kept walking. I heard a burst of laughter coming from behind me as I passed the house. My sister not only had a smart mouth, she never let me forget the fact that she was one year older, and three grades ahead and smarter than me.

Quickly my thoughts returned back to my destination, the party, which from a distance appeared to be going on strong, but when I arrived in the driveway I noticed the police were trying to disperse the crowd. I could overhear a group of girls complaining as they were leaving, that one of the neighbors had called the police on them because of the noise and the rowdy behavior, and the fact alcohol was being served to minors.

I saw Rob and J.C. in the crowd as they were headed out of the driveway, and we walked down the street for a moment headed for a '76 Buick Park Avenue that Jeff, Rob's cousin occasionally let him drive. Rob was the only one of us that actually had his license. We had all been drinking that night and we drove around. J.C. and some girl he met at the party were necking in the back seat, while we parked, talked to some girls and drank beer. About two in the morning I was ready to go home. I don't know why, but I told Rob to let me off at the corner of my street. I was staggering down the street hoping to make it home before my mother or grandmother saw me.

Chapter 2

I woke up the next morning with the liquor I'd consumed the night before stale on my breath, my clothes, and shoes still on. I felt my mother hovering over my bed. Now my mother is not the smallest women in the world, she's a towering 5'9". I tried to sit up, at the same time wondering how I got into the bed in the first place. The last thing I remembered was staggering down the street to get home.

"You're just like your father," I heard my mother say as I looked up and the glare of the sunlight hit my eyes, with one hand propping me up, and the other trying to shield my eyes from the glare, me squinting as I looked up. The fact that she mentioned my father caught me by surprise.

"Do you know how you got home?" she said, looking at me with disgust.

"Yeah, I remember," I said, trying not to let her know I didn't. "Sort of," I added so I wouldn't be caught lying.

"Sort of? Either you do or you don't. Was Carla with you and Rob and J.C. while you all were out drinking and carryin on?"

I had to think for a minute, *Was she?*... then I remembered. "No, I walked her home before I went with them."

"Thank you, Jesus. I go to church with her mother and father. And the last thing I need for you to do is to make me look bad in front of her parents and embarrass me in front of the whole congregation at church." I rolled my eyes. "Look, mister," she said, "I don't know who you are rolling your eyes at, or where you're getting your ways from, but you didn't learn 'em here, that's for sure." She started for the door and I thought that the speech over, but it wasn't.

She turned back around. "How much liquor did you drink, 'cause I can still smell it all over your breath."

I opened my mouth, and I started to lie, and then I closed it, because I knew she would catch me lying, so I looked up at her and then burst out laughing.

"I don't see anything funny. I asked you a question, boy, and I want you to answer it."

I knew she was serious, but I couldn't help grinning at her. I thought about the question, the truth would be I drank a lot, and a lie would be that I didn't know, so I was left with, "I don't remember," an answer, which was where the truth and a lie coincide, even though it may have been closer to the truth than even I realized.

She sighed putting her hands on her hips and said, "I'm sick of your mess," and headed out of my room into the hallway.

This time as she left she was ranting and raving as she headed towards the stairs.

"You think this is a joke." I could hear her still yelling as she was going down the steps. "You are not leaving this house today or for the whole summer since everything's so funny. I'm here to remind you. I'm still the adult and you are still the child. You are not getting on that phone, and I don't want anyone in this house, now I mean that and I mean for the entire summer, do you understand?"

All I could do is yell back "okay." I know she heard me because I heard her stop midway on the stairs and then say, "Now, laugh at that!"

Before I got a chance to sit up on my bed and recuperate from the conversation I just had with my mother, my sister peeked in the room.

"What do you want?" I asked.

"Grandma said breakfast is ready. Mama's going to get ready for work, and we're havin' bacon and eggs. Hurry up!" Then she disappeared smiling as she left. I leaned on the side of my bed holding my stomach, sick from thought of bacon and eggs. I tried breathing deeply, I couldn't figure out whether it was the bacon or the eggs that made me the more nauseous. Unable to hold back the puke, I ran to the bathroom and vomited. The smell of the food coming up the steps made me sicker, I heaved about three or four more times, praying to God if he would make me feel better I'd never drink like that again. I stopped when I felt better. I even tested myself by standing up straight, my stomach was still queasy and I heaved a couple of more times. After that I was able to stand up without feeling sick to my stomach. It was over; I flushed the toilet and rinsed my mouth.

ANGELS ONLY STAND
WHERE CHERUBIM TAKE FLIGHT

I stood in the mirror admiring my physique. I joked, thinking to myself, *Boy you are really handsome*. I had muscles, brown skin, muscles, nice afro, mustache, and my goatee beginning to grow in. I was standing in the mirror playing around by chanting, "Sam, Sam, Sam, I'm the ladies' man," dancing, and bobbing my head up and down at the same time.

After I finished fooling around in the bathroom mirror, I decided to take a shower. When I got out, I dried off and took the towel and wrapped it around my waist like the man in the shaving commercials, and headed down the hallway to my room. I placed my dirty clothes in the hamper and looked for an album I could listen to. I'd bought that stereo for fifteen dollars, from a fellow in school. I made the speakers myself, a great accomplishment that I was very proud of. Since she didn't mention that I couldn't listen to any music, I thought, *Well it's going to be a long summer....* I wasn't hungry so I placed the record on the turntable and when the music started I began dancing, with the towel wrapped around my waist, in one place. Then I walked over to my window and opened it. I looked out to see if any of my friends were out there. No, just some kids riding bikes in the street. I decided to go get some juice, but I was afraid my of having to face my grandmother. I took my head out the window and closed it half way, put on my clothes, and went downstairs. There she was, my grandmother. I think I would have been more comfortable in front of an execution squad.

"Jerry?"

Here it comes, I thought. "Yes, Grandma?"

"Pastor Brown called, since you're out for the summer, he would like to know if you want to work. You could earn some earn extra money."

"Doing what?" I asked while looking for the orange juice.

"Mowin' lawns, pullin' weeds." I turned around to face her, this isn't the conversation I imagined having with her. She was smiling, pointing over towards the stove.

"There some biscuits there on top of the stove and some bacon in the oven."

"When does he want me to start?" I asked.

"Tomorrow morning at six o'clock."

"Okay, Grandma."

"You go down to the church in the morning, you tell Jimmy you are Sister White's grandson."

"Who is Jimmy?" I asked, because it was the first time I had heard of him.

"Oh, he's our youth choir director and he has his own landscaping business, maybe if you come to church sometime you can meet his family."

His daughter, she meant. The girls of the world that I brought home weren't good enough for her. She felt my future wife needed to have a good church upbringing.

"Okay," I told her as I sipped on my juice. I resented the idea that she was playing matchmaker, because the memory of the last date I botched was still fresh in my mind.

"You know, work will make a good man out of you. It'll keep you out of trouble. It won't hurt you one bit." Then she started that "when I was young" stuff. I turned my head and mimicked her silently. "When I was young, we worked hard, we lived on a farm, we didn't have it as easy as you all do today. This is a bunch of spoiled kids coming up today, yes Lord."

"Grandma," I said interrupting her, "do you have five dollars so I can buy lunch tomorrow?"

"What's wrong with making your lunch? Granny needs her five dollars to put in church this Sunday."

"Well can you make it? Please, Granny?"

I put on my famous begging face, the kind I knew she couldn't refuse.

"I guess so," she said.

"Thanks, Grandma." I kissed her on the cheek and ran upstairs, I had a job for the summer. Money. I'd get my driver's license and buy a car.

I got up the next morning at five. I was just buttering a couple of slices of toast when I heard Mama upstairs getting up for work also. I sat eating my toast, dunking it in orange juice, a habit I learned from my sister. After breakfast I took my lunch out of the refrigerator, which was in a small brown bag. I looked inside, there was a one-dollar bill laying at the bottom underneath my sandwiches. I took it out and put the money in my jean pocket. As I was leaving I heard my mother coming down the steps. "Have a good day a work," her voice coming from behind me.

"Okay, bye Mama."

"Bye son, don't forget you're still on punishment, when you get home you stay home."

"Okay, Mama."

I left the house and headed up the street to the church on Ninety-third and there in the parking lot were four other boys waiting. I stood and waited too and then I saw an older gentleman coming out of the church. He glanced at me and seemed puzzled.

"Hi, I'm Sister White's grandson."

ANGELS ONLY STAND
WHERE CHERUBIM TAKE FLIGHT

He smiled. "Oh yeah, hi, I'm Brother Atkinson, but you can call me Jimmy." He offered me his hand and I shook it.

"Okay," he said, "we have someone new. Come over here, Jeremiah, I want to introduce you to the other boys. Jeremiah this is Troy, Jose, Derek, and Malachi."

We all greeted each other shaking hands, then all of us except for Jose sat in the truck bed, Jose sat in the front with Jimmy. We drove out to a small restaurant and mowed the lawn and trimmed the hedges, pulling weeds if we saw them. I noticed some of the workers putting out umbrellas on the tables and cleaning off the chairs. I thought that the people who ate here probably had a lot of money. I imagined as I worked that businessmen and lawyers got together here to have lunch with their women or people they do business with. They would open probably soon after we left.

We went to a recreation center next, then a daycare and finally a funeral home. We were packing up the lawnmowers on the trailers and Jimmy stopped and asked me how I liked my day.

"It was a lot of hard work, my feet hurt, but the funeral home reminded me of my father," I told him.

"Yeah, the funeral home brings bad memories for me, too. But the work, you'll get used to it. Just be lucky you have a grandmother who cares a great deal about you and a strong mother who loves you."

Jimmy dropped us all off at home, I was the second one he dropped off. I got out of the back of the truck and started for the porch steps. My grandmother stood waving to Jimmy.

"Okay, Sister White, I'll be seeing you." Grandmother stood smiling.

"Did you know Brother Atkinson works part-time as a policeman?"

"No, I didn't." I watched my grandmother staring at the truck as it drove off. I turned and watched also, as Jimmy headed up the street. The first thing I did when I got into the house was to take a soak in the tub. I went into my room and turned on the fan. I was asleep in no time. I had a busy day tomorrow and I needed my rest.

I worked the entire summer. Just like Jimmy had told me, I got used to the work. He was a pretty cool person for a cop. He said he'd help me obtain my driver's license when I told him how old I was. He made a comment to me how every sixteen-year-old should have his driver's license, whether they were on punishment or not. I studied for my temporary driver's license for two weeks before I took the test. It was Saturday and Jimmy came to pick me up.

"Nervous?" he asked.

I grinned. "A little."

"Well, just think of it this way; after you get your temporary, you can prepare to get your driver's license."

I nodded my head to let him know I understood. I couldn't wait to catch up with my friends, they all had their licenses.

When we arrived at the license bureau, I wandered inside ahead of Jimmy, there were three lines, one for people who wanted to renew their licenses or I.D.s and second was for people waiting to take the driver's test. The third line was for temporary licenses which was where I belonged. I looked behind me for Jimmy and signaled to him that I was going over to the desk.

When I walked to the desk, there were two other people ahead of me but the line went fast. I saw them pay their money and take a paper where they were directed the side of the room where they were to take their test.

When I came up to the desk, I told him I was there to take my temporary license test. I paid six dollars and was given a test. He directed me to the side of the room with the others.

Now the test was a little easier than I thought it would be, however that was the first part. I think the most trouble I had was with the signs. I completed my test and took my test back to the man that stood behind the desk. He check off the questions I got wrong. I got a 97%; I passed. I breathed a breath of relief as he told me. Then he had me look through something that looked like a pair of binoculars. He asked me, did I see certain things and what color and what were they? I gave my answers, I passed the visual part. Then I was issued my temporary license. I went to where Jimmy was sitting; I was so proud.

"I got 97% on the test," I said smiling.

"I'll be able to take you out to practice driving after work," he said.

"Okay." I was happy that someone was finally taking interest in me.

"You want to go out now, just so you can see what it's like?"

"Yeah."

"Okay."

I was itching to get behind the wheel. When Jimmy drove to the parking lot, I told him, "I know how to drive a little bit because my friend taught me to drive his."

"All right, well, let's see what you've got."

I took my seat behind the wheel and drove. I was surprised I hadn't forgotten how to do it. I remember when Rob taught J.C. and I how to drive.

ANGELS ONLY STAND
WHERE CHERUBIM TAKE FLIGHT

I remember when Rob stole his mother's car one night. We all had been drinking and he had gotten so drunk that he asked me to drive his mother's car home. We got caught that night by Rob's mother and of course my mother and my grandmother heard about it the next day. I'll never forget the look on their faces. It's one thing to get in trouble and have to face your mother, but having to face your grandmother also, that's even harder.

I turned the corner, leading out of the parking lot, and went down the street. I showed off a little driving through the neighborhood as people watched. Jimmy told me to drive home and told me I had taken all the joy out of him helping me learn how to drive. He said, "It's like teaching your son to ride a bike and then discovering he already knows how and doesn't need your help."

"Thanks anyway, Dad."

My mother was standing on the porch when I pulled up at home.

On my job I made five dollars an hour, a good salary. Since I didn't have to pay rent or buy groceries, I saved my money to buy a car. Jimmy still gave me driving lessons. He said he could still teach me something even though I handled myself pretty good behind the wheel, so he would take me out, and while I was learning, I saved money for a car.

The day I got my license marked a day of high achievement for me. After I had worked the whole summer, I had managed to save enough money to buy a used '76 Ninety-eight. I had Jimmy take me to the lot where his friend worked. I got out of the car and went over to the parked Ninety-eight. I cupped my hands and looked inside the windows; it was maroon and it had white leather interior. I asked him like I always did, "How much?"

"For you, since you're a friend of a friend, one thousand five hundred," he said.

I talked to Jimmy and said, "I have the money, can you take me to the bank?" Jimmy took me to the bank, so when I came back I simply bought it; it was clean and had good mileage. I didn't have the car five minutes before I told Jimmy I was going over to show it off to Rob and J.C. I hoped they would be home. I remember the last time I had seen them was the night I got drunk. It was September 1, I had been on punishment since June, and I was off now. I drove past the grocery store where a group of girls where standing. I thought I knew one of the girls, but I wasn't sure. I kept on driving up to the street where Rob lived. He and J.C. and his brother Curtis were sitting on the front porch talking with music blaring. I pulled into the driveway. Rob laughed when he saw me.

"What's up, Jerry?" They greeted me, giving me five as they gathered around the car, teasing that I was finally off punishment.

"Who's car is this, Jerry?"

"It's mine. I bought it today. See I got the thirty-day tags." I pointed to the rear window. "C'mon, get in, I'm going up the street. There's a bunch of girls sitting out in front of the store. I know one of them." I pulled out of the driveway driving off onto the main road.

As we approached the store, I could hear J.C. arguing with his brother over the girls they would meet in the back seat. I drove past slowly until I saw the girl I thought I knew, then I pulled into the parking lot. The girls came over to the car when Rob, Curtis and J.C. had gotten out. They had already begun talking to them. I got out going to the other side of the car where the girl that I knew was standing, dressed in a pair of jeans and heels; her hair was feathered back and her skin was a chestnut brown. As I came up behind her, I tapped her gently on the shoulder. "Hi," I said as she turned around, she looked sort of startled. "Aren't you Annette's cousin?" Annette was a girl that Rob used to date. "I met you before, my name is Jeremiah. You remember me, don't you?"

"Yes, I remember you."

"What's your name again?"

"Denise," she answered with a smile on her face.

"Yeah, um," I said looking around. "Denise, where's your cousin?"

She pointed into the crowd, my eyes followed her finger and I saw her cousin. Then I looked at the crowd and J.C. had my radio on, turned up full blast, break dancing on a piece of cardboard in the middle of the parking lot. I turned and looked at her.

"Look," I asked her, "Do you have a boyfriend, Denise?"

I hoped she wouldn't lie. The last thing I needed was for some other fellow to come out of nowhere mad because I'm talking to his lady. She shook her head no.

"Let me give you my phone number and you can call me if you want. I got a job and that's my car over there." I took out a piece of bubble gum from out of my pocket, stuck the gum in my mouth and wrote my number on the empty wrapper. Even though I was young, I tried my best to impress her.

"Don't you have a sister?" she asked. "April? She's a senior up at John Adams."

"Yes, I do. Everybody knows my sister."

All of a sudden, we were interrupted; the police came by and said we couldn't loiter in the parking lot.

"Call me later," I said to Denise as she and her friends began to walk down the street. My friends and I got into the car. I drove over to my house taking the long way. When we got to my house, we sat on the porch. It was hot that afternoon and my mother was just getting home.

"I'll see you tomorrow, Georgia."

Mrs. Ivory picked my mother up and dropped her off every day for work. She lived a block away. I think she might have helped Mama find that job at the cleaners.

"Good evening, boys," Mama said as she made her way up the stairs.

"Hi, Mrs. Washington," Rob and J.C. said in unison.

"Hi, Ma."

"Jeremiah, go on inside and get you and your friends some pie and ice cream if you want."

Rob, Curtis and J.C. looked at me. Rob was rubbing his hands together. "You heard what your mama said, boy, go get us some pie and ice cream!"

As I got up and proceeded to go inside, I turned and said to my friends, "You coming in? 'Cause I'm not a waiter."

They all followed me into the house. We got our plates and went back to our chairs on the porch.

"Mmm, this pie is good."

"Hey, Jeremiah, you think if I married your mama she'd cook like this for me?" J.C. asked.

"Man, you better not try it," I answered him.

"What's the matter, son, then he'd be your daddy," Rob said laughing.

"Forget you all, man. My mother is not thinking about none of ya'll."

"Does Francis cooks like this?" Rob asked.

"The only thing Francis knows how to do is spend money. Ain't that right, J.C.?" I answered.

"No, J.C. is the player, right? He ain't got no job. Francis do," Curtis said.

"Right, right," Rob and I echoed.

"He spends her money," Rob replied.

"And Jeremiah over there ain't got no woman; his mother will pass the recipe to his sister. Right? She can put on those sexy draws your mama caught her wit and come over my house and cook for me. Ain't that right, Jerry?" Curtis said joking of course.

"Man, You ain't touchin' my sister or my mother, understand?"

We were all laughing.

"I'll tell you what, though, if your mother ever wanted to come over here and give it a go, she can feel what it's like to have a real man. Oops, I forgot to tell you, I'm your daddy, anyway, man." I put my hand out for Rob to shake it with a smile on my face.

We joked like this all the time; he didn't shake it, of course. Curtis was the only one to slap my hand, jumping up and down in his seat. "Good one, good one," he repeated, almost choking on his food from laughing so hard.

"Man, you and Curtis can go to hell. My—," and then he stopped. When I looked at Rob he appeared to be awe struck, mouth hanging open as if he saw a ghost. We all looked up and there was Mama.

"I told you all I don't want you all cusssin' on my front porch. Now I know you don't go home and cuss in your houses, do you?"

"No."

"And Jerry, I just know you weren't standin' here on my front porch cussin', now were you?"

"No, Mama, I didn't even say nothin'." She looked at me as if to say, *You better had not been.*

"How did you all like the pie?"

"It was good, Mrs. Washington," they said in unison.

"Why don't you boys go on back and pick me a basket full of pears and pick me some greens, Jeremiah. Go in and get them some gloves.

I went to the basement, where I managed to get the gloves that didn't have holes in them. There where several pair, I took four. I brought the gloves upstairs to Rob and J.C and Curtis and led the way out the side door into the backyard.

I said, "J.C., you wanna pick the greens with me? Rob and Curtis can pick the pears."

I took the step ladder out of the garage and placed it next to the tree. When J.C. and I were picking the greens, Rob yelled down, "Can we get a basket of pears?"

"Okay," I answered.

I finished picking Mama's greens and placed them into a bag. It was hot so we all went inside to get some water, after that I got another basket so that we could pick some more pears.

"Jeremiah," I could hear Mama yelling from upstairs, "get Mrs. Campbell and Mrs. Elliott some tomatoes and cucumbers."

So I went back outside and while they picked the pears, I picked the tomatoes and cucumbers, placing them in a bag. When we finished, we went back inside. Mama was in the kitchen sitting in fresh clothes.

"We're getting ready to go, Ma. I'm taking them home."

"Okay. Rob and James, you make sure you tell your mothers about the revival at our church this week. Jeremiah, did you give your friends the tomatoes and cucumbers for their mothers?"

Oh yeah, I had forgotten in that short period of time. I handed them the bags and we made our way out the door.

"Thank you, Mrs. Washington."

"You boys have a good day, stay out of trouble."

"We will, Mama."

We got in the car and I turned the music up and drove out of the driveway up the street.

"Let's get some beer," J.C. said.

"No, not today, in this car. I'm not going home drunk," quickly remembering that I had been on punishment all summer. "Besides, I got to go home, take this trash out, and Denise is calling tonight."

"Well, let's go to the store and drop us off over Rob's," J.C. said.

"Okay." I stopped at the store while Rob went in and purchased the beer, besides having his license he had a fake I.D.

When he got back in the car, J.C. asked me, "So you talking to Denise?"

"Yeah, you ever date her?"

"Nope, but she used to mess with this dude. His name is Rufus; he's a senior up at Adams."

"I think I know who you're talking about. My sister knows him. He used to like her. Well, just as long as you haven't messed with her, I guess I will talk to her. With all the girls you mess with, you just better be glad that Francis hasn't found out."

"Yeah, 'cause she will beat the daylights out of him," Rob said. "Remember the dance?" he added. Rob and I began to laugh. I pulled up to Rob's house and they got out.

"Okay, Jerry, man." J.C placed his hand on my shoulder, and said, "Hurry home to your woman," as he laughed.

"She's not my lady yet, man."

"All right, partner," Rob said. We did our brotherly handshakes and I left, going back home. I took the trash out and retreated to my room to wait for Denise to call.

It was still a couple weeks before school started. I was entering the tenth grade even though I was supposed to be in the eleventh. Denise however was in the tenth, also. She was one year younger than me.

She finally called that evening. I talked to her for hours. Even my mother came to my room, looking at me strangely. We talked as if we knew each other all our young lives. After I told her I'd call her back, if she didn't mind, we hung up. I couldn't quite understand it. Did we have that much in common, or was I infatuated with her? After courting her over the phone for about a month, I invited her to the amusement park, Geauga Lake. I was nervous. I hadn't been on a date without my buddies Rob and J.C. simply because I didn't have a car. We would often double date, Rob and I, since it was quite clear to most of the girls that J.C. already had a steady girlfriend. When I picked her up, I tried not to stare at her, because when I looked at her, I couldn't believe that she was just fifteen. She looked so much older than that. I mean, if I had to guess, I think she looked about eighteen or seventeen years old. I on the other hand, didn't look like that young myself. I appeared much older than just sixteen. We pulled into the parking lot at the park.

We walked around the park, rode the roller coasters, ate corn dogs and fries and at the end of the evening I took her to my car. We sat for about three hours just talking. I asked her if she would be my lady and when she said yes the fireworks exploded in my mind. My head was in the clouds and as the fog began to lift, as our lips parted, I regained my strength and started the car and drove out of the empty parking lot. She accompanied me like a singer is accompanied by a symphony. I never had a better time.

When I dropped her off, it was about 2:00 in the morning. I saw her inside and spoke to her mother and we said our goodbyes and I drove home.

Mama hadn't forgot about me either. When school started, I guess Jimmy had a conversation with her and they decided to talk to my school's principal about excelling me to my proper grade. I tested into regular classes that year, but I still had to attend special classes for math. The principal, Mrs. Thatcher thought it would be a good idea also to have me to go to summer school so I could graduate in 1979 like the rest of my friends. I would have to go to night school, also. I agreed I would do this, so each Saturday after work I attended a class. It's not quite the school year I imagined. I had a lot of hard work, no time to spend with Denise, but Jimmy encouraged me, telling me he thought it was necessary to help build my self-esteem.

Meanwhile, my sister was graduating from high school this June, not to mention she received a full scholarship to go to Kent State University. Mama was so proud of her. All Mama would talk about was how "April is going to college" and how she received "a full scholarship to go to Kent to earn a degree in teaching."

ANGELS ONLY STAND
WHERE CHERUBIM TAKE FLIGHT

She sounded more like the town crier; whenever she ran into any of her friends, especially in the stores, she would really carry on. The way she sounded, you'd think she was the one going. Taking up to a half an hour of people's time, rambling about the same thing she might have told them last week. I guess I was a little bit jealous. I also realized it is special when a young black teenage girl goes away to college, especially when they're the first of the family to go. That could call for a special occasion. I guess that's why people didn't mind sitting and listening to her brag.

One particular day, I had just gotten off work. I went to visit Denise. I sat in a chair with her standing behind me, my car parked in the driveway as she braided my hair. She had the music on her favorite disco station. I, on the other hand, was not into disco I liked R&B. As she braided my hair, I noticed a fellow on a bicycle making his way up the driveway. He got off the bike and walked it past my car, being careful not to scratch it, then he made his way up the path, up the stairs and onto Denise's front porch. "What's up, Denise?"

"I'm braiding my boyfriend's hair," she answered.

He offered his hand to me. "What's up, man? I'm Rufus."

"Jeremiah." We shook hands.

"Like the one in the Bible, right?"

I detected he was poking fun at me. "Right," I said.

"So you're Denise's new boyfriend?"

"Yeah," I answered.

"I used to go with her," he answered.

"Rufus, will you please go away? Can't you see I have company?"

"Oh I have to leave? I thought you wanted me to meet your boyfriend, least that's what you told me the other day."

"Look, man, she wants you to go."

Rufus looked at me and Denise, laughing as he pointed to both of us. "Oh, right, it's you and her now. All right, man, I'm gone." He went to the bottom of the stairs, picked up his bicycle and mounted it. "I'll see you tomorrow, Denise." He rode off down the driveway into the street. I watched as he got to the end of the street and turned the corner and disappeared. I was relieved.

"He's a simpleton," Denise said as she continued to braid my hair.

"What did he mean he'd be back tomorrow?" I asked. I had to admit I was a little jealous.

"Like I said, he's a simpleton, he just said it 'cause he's simpleminded."

"Oh." I realized that she was probably right. I mean, she did introduce me as her boyfriend, maybe he wanted me to think there was something more going on.

"He must still like you."

"He was my boyfriend in the eight grade."

"Oh, so he's just a friend?" She detected my jealousy, that's when she stuck the comb in my hair and she came and stood in front of me.

"Yes, I can have friends, can't I?" I began to get upset so I explained to her, "You can have all the friends you want as long as I can have them, too. It's not like we're married."

After I made that statement, I saw Denise's facial expression change.

"You want me to finish your hair?"

"Yes. Why, you don't want to?"

"Maybe one of your friends can finish it."

"What's wrong with you? You have your ex-boyfriend come over and then all of a sudden you start buggin' out, all bent out of shape because I told you I have friends, too."

"You don't have to get so upset."

"Look, girl," I told her, "if I want to play games, I'll buy a Monopoly board." I stood up and took my comb out of my half-done hair and placed it in my back pocket. "I'm gone. I'll call you later."

I walked down her front steps and got into my car turned my music on till it was blasting. Still angry, I went home, thinking about the nerve she had to tell me to let one of my friends finish doing my hair. I pulled into the driveway and went into the house, unconsciously slamming the front screen. I went through the kitchen headed straight for the refrigerator. I opened the refrigerator and pulled out a cold can of ginger ale and put it on my forehead, that's when I heard Mama say, "Can't you speak?"

I took the can off my head and looked over.

"Hi," I answered.

"What's wrong with you?" she asked.

"What do you mean?"

"You came in here with an attitude slamming doors. You were probably so angry you didn't even see me sitting here. And what's with your head?"

"I got in a argument with my girlfriend."

"Oh, so now you've got a girlfriend."

"Well, yeah."

"What's her name?"

"Denise."

ANGELS ONLY STAND
WHERE CHERUBIM TAKE FLIGHT

If it's one thing I didn't like, it's to talk to my mother about my personal business. I'd rather be talking to my grandmother only because she was more understanding.

"What type of argument did you get in?"

"About having friends."

"See, Jeremiah, that's why you need to watch being with these girls. You all get too serious too early."

"Mama, I'm not serious."

"That's what I mean. My mother wouldn't let me date till I was sixteen." I looked at my mother thinking to myself, *And you still married a jerk.*

"You aren't mature enough yet to have a girlfriend," she continued. "A girl becomes your steady girlfriend if you all plan on marrying, not that 'I'll have her as a girlfriend, and then if we break up, hey, I can find someone else.'"

"Mama, I am sixteen."

"Well, I bet she isn't."

"Times are different now. Why are you so concerned anyway?"

"Because the Lord didn't intend for people to behave this way, that's why. Having one girlfriend after another, and are you having sex with this girl, Jeremiah?" I stood at the end of the table I hadn't even opened up the ginger ale. I was afraid to answer the question.

There was a lump in my throat. "Yes," I answered.

"You know what, just go," she said waving her hand up in the air.

"Why?"

"Just get out of my face, I am not going to even waste my breath. If you want to live your life full of chaos and sin, go right on ahead."

"My life isn't full of chaos."

"Well, she already doesn't want you to have friends, it's not like you put a six hundred dollar wedding ring on her finger. Or were you that stupid?"

"No, Ma, I told her that—."

"Go."

"But Ma—."

"Go on, Jeremiah."

"You wont even let me speak up for myself."

"When you have something intelligent for me to hear, that's when I'll listen, so just go on out of here. I don't want to hear that buggy-eyed bull crap you talk."

I started towards the living room to the stairs. "If anyone calls me, I'm asleep." I was tired, I lay across my bed, thinking of the conversation I had with Mama.

School would not start for another couple of days. I took Denise and myself and bought some clothes for school. His and her tee shirts, look-alike jackets, anyhow I had dropped Denise off at her house. My grandmother greeted me on the front porch as I was coming up the steps with my bags.

"Anything for me in those bags?" she asked smiling.

"Hi, Grandma," I said as I sat the bags down.

"I hear you have a new girlfriend." I thought to myself, *Word travels fast in this house*.

"Yeah," I answered, "we just went shopping."

"How much money do you have left?"

"A couple of dollars. I'll make it till payday."

"Jeremiah, you need to start setting some money aside for college. You do plan on going, don't you?"

"Yes, Grandma, I do want to go."

That's how I started saving for college. Jimmy taught me to make a ledger and put all my earnings in it. First decide what to spend my money on, then decide how much I wanted to spend. I learned to record every dime that I would spend on clothes, gas, lunch, and how much I would set aside for college.

Chapter 3

September 9, the first day of school rolled around; I picked Denise up for school. Every day we would argue in the morning about what radio station that we would listen to, disco or R&B. I told her, "This is my car and when you get your car you can listen to whatever you want. I don't want people to hear the Village People's 'Macho Man' coming from my car and that's that." Truth is, I would have let her listen to any station she wanted to but I saw the arguing as a kind of a game, a power struggle we'd play, the kind I had needed at that time to win.

It was three weeks before I turned eighteen. The hallways were decorated and I was walking to class and thinking about Denise and how were going to get together for the weekend and go to the movies. Everything was normal as far as I could tell. I was minding my business and I turned around because I thought I heard someone talking to me.

There were a few students loitering in the hall. And I saw this someone walking up towards me the size of a football player. It was Rufus. So I asked him if he was talking to me and I looked at him. He had on a baseball cap, cocked to the side, a jean jacket that covered a dirty tee-shirt, a pair of jeans that looked as if his knees had been sitting in dirt and a worn out pair of black sneakers and he was staggering like he was drunk or high or something, then he said, "Do you all read Dick and Jane books in that class you goin' to?" He was laughing as he said it.

"What are you talking about?" I asked nervously because I could hear the students in the hallway burst out into laughter and I could feel myself get hot.

All of a sudden he rushed up to me pulled me by the collar of my shirt yelling, "I don't like you, man. You're a punk, man, a retard." Then he stood back opened his jacket and lunged at me with a knife and started to push me and plunged the knife on the side of my shoulder. The next thing I knew we were fighting. He punched me in the face and my lip began to bleed. I looked for a weapon; I grabbed the thing closest to me which was a chair. I was scared so at that moment I decided I was going to try and knock the knife out of his hand. I took the chair and I hit him just below the shoulder and the knife fell, then he tried to lunged at my legs to make me fall, but somehow I managed to jump back and he missed my legs and hit the floor.

By this time teachers had come out of the classrooms and broken us up, students flooded the hallway, and the principal Mrs. Thatcher and assistant principal Mrs. Jones were pulling me by the arm over to the side of the hallway. I stood trying to catch my breath while they attended to Rufus, he lay on the floor until the ambulance came. Then the paramedics came and placed him on to the gurney and took him to the hospital. The police helped me onto the other gurney and escorted me to the hospital asking me all types of questions on the way to the hospital. I told them how the fight started, that he had started it first by talking about Dick and Jane books and then by calling me retarded. I also told them he had a knife and he pulled it out on me twice and stabbed me in my shoulder. I told them that I had grabbed the chair that was in the hallway and started to knock the knife out of his hand, because I didn't want to get killed. The police asked me did I know about Rufus liking or having a relationship with my girlfriend Denise. I told the police I didn't think Denise was seeing him and he might of have liked her or maybe he was jealous of me because I had a car, a job, and besides, Denise was no bad-looking young lady. Rumors were already flying about him liking Denise or something like that.

Chapter 4

I arrived at the emergency room and received ten stitches in my shoulder. I sat waiting on the examination table when the doctor said he would return with my prescription for a pain reliever. Ten minutes later a nurse came in and told me that there were some officers waiting and that they wanted to see me. After she left they came in the room, before I realized what was happening, they told me I was under arrest for murder. They read me my rights, and took me out of the emergency room with my arms handcuffed behind me. When I tried to tell them I was waiting for my mother and grandmother, they told me that the hospital would inform them as to what had happened to me. Rufus had died on the way to the hospital. However, that wasn't the problem. My problem was that the police claimed they found no weapon on or around Rufus and made the claims that I unmercifully beat Rufus with a chair. I told the police that he did stab me; they made claims that maybe one of his rings caused the gash in my shoulder and arm. This couldn't be happening, I thought. The last thing I needed was for my mother and grandmother to think that I murdered someone. I wished something ironic like lightning would strike me down dead, to me that was better than facing my mother.

People stood watching as I got into the squad car. The police then got into the front and drove off. We were on the main road when a call came through. After that he pulled into a vacant lot. Both officers got out off the car. I sat wondering what was going on until he open the car door to the back seat where I was sitting and one of the officers said, "Get out."

"Excuse me?" I answered.

"Get out of the car," he repeated.

I began to scoot down the back seat to get out of the vehicle, I felt the air hit my face, I stood up.

"Now," he said, "it's very important that we get all the facts. Right, Officer Johnson?"

"Yes," the other officer repeated, "it's important we get all the facts."

His partner then looked at me and said, "Son, I want you to think hard and tell us exactly what happened this afternoon."

I began to rehearse the events as they unfolded. "I was walking down the hallway and Rufus began to make fun of me because I was in special classes. He began to push me and flashed a knife. That's when the fight broke out, that's when he stabbed me. I picked up a chair and knocked the knife out of his hand. I didn't beat him. And that's what happened."

The first officer leaned over my shoulder and spoke into my ear. "No, that's not what happened."

"That is what happened, honestly, Officer. I—."

"I don't think you heard me, son. I said that is not what happened."

I was silent.

His partner Officer Johnson took his stick and hit me across the back of my knees. I buckled and fell on the ground, my hands still cuffed in back of me.

He stood me up.

He leaned over my shoulder and spoke again, saying, "Now that's not what happened, now is it?"

I remained silent. He punched me in my stomach twice. I bent over so he couldn't punch me in my stomach again, but he pulled my head up and punched me again. I could feel him lift me up as I bent over again, this time because of the pain.

"Now," he said, "I'm going to tell you what happened. You started the fight and you beat an innocent person to death, because he liked your girlfriend, isn't that right?"

"No," I insisted, "he had a knife. I was just—."

The officer took his hand around my neck and choked me, then he punched me in my stomach and pushed me to the ground. They began kicking me and beating me with their sticks and when I began to shout, the first officer picked me up by my afro.

"He didn't have a knife, did he, son? You just made the whole thing up. You beat an innocent man to death."

The tears that were forming in my eyes made it so I couldn't see, and I was staggering.

"That's what happened, right, boy?" He took the stick and raised it in front of my face. I put my face down and before he hit me I broke down.

"Yes, yes. I killed him on purpose." The stick hit the squad car after I spoke.

He laughed and said, "That sounds like a confession to me," he said to the other officer.

"That's right," the second officer repeated.

"All right, son, all we wanted was the truth. Before you get into the car, you need to sign this statement and then we'll let you back in the car."

They took the handcuffs off my hands and I have never been so eager to sign something in my life. I didn't even read it; all I wanted was to go to prison so they couldn't beat me anymore. The police watched as I placed my signature down on the paper he held in his hand. He was laughing as he placed the handcuffs back on me. When I got down to the center, I really was at a loss for words because I was in shock. My life was taking a turn in a direction where I really didn't want to go. Needless to say I received a uniform, and toiletries and a brief orientation about how things were going to be run there.

The first night there I couldn't sleep, I stayed up the whole night. I wanted my mother. I wished this were some kind of nightmare and in the morning things would be different. I wanted to be at home in my own bed.

The first person I saw was my lawyer. I had one provided to me by the court. Her name was Miss Lipinski, a petite women with a gentle but firm voice and thin brown hair. She discussed my case with me. She asked me how I slept. I told her not too good, trying careful not to go into great detail about my sleep. I began to tell her about the police hitting me. "They said you gave them a hard time."

"They're lying, Miss Lipinski."

"Police don't lie. Did anyone see them?"

"No, but—."

"Can you prove it?"

"No."

"Look, Mr. Washington, I can't build a case against the police. You have murdered someone. That has a lot to say about your credibility."

"But I didn't do it on purpose," I pleaded.

She raised her voice waving the paper in my face. "I have a signed statement from you that you confessed to premeditated murder. Look, they are seeking to try you as an adult. The best way I can help you, Mr. Washington, is to see that that does not happen. Now they are going to have an arraignment. There they will decide the date of your pre-trial and then, maybe you could go home with your mother if the court decided this would be in your best interest." After she left I went back to my unit. It was recreation time when I came back and a fellow I had made friends with named Johnny asked me did I want to play cards with him and a couple of other fellows. So I sat down and played a couple of rounds with them, after we finished we talked.

"Why are you here, Jerry?" he asked.

"I got into a fight," I told him.

"You kill someone?"

"Why?" I asked.

"Just because there's this story everywhere on the news, on all the channels. John Adams, right?"

"I didn't do it, and besides, he had a knife."

"Yeah, but did you know his uncle was a cop?"

At first I didn't make the connection, I didn't care. I opened my mouth ignorantly.

"What does that have to do with anything?" And then it ran again. The newscaster was sitting in the newsroom and a picture of my school in the far right corner, and then they flashed to a scene where his uncle who, unfortunately for me, served at the ninth district, was telling the newscaster that I brutally murdered his nephew and how the courts should show no mercy on me and I should be tried as an adult. The whole city was riled up. I just sat back and assessed the situation. I imagined if I were on the news, how could I politely remind him his innocent nephew attacked me first? He pulled the knife out on me. He was the one trying to kill me. I was just defending myself.

"Man, you're going to burn."

I couldn't understand why Johnny said that. He knew something I didn't. I just kept everything he said in mind, then to lighten up things I changed the conversation. I asked him why he was here.

"I was following my girlfriend around."

"You were stalking your girlfriend?"

"I thought she was seeing someone else behind my back."

"But if she was, man, why didn't you just ask her?"

"I jumped on her and her parents filed a complaint on me, so I went over there trying to smooth things out, you know, tell her that I loved her, and I wouldn't hit her again."

"And what did she say?"

"She didn't say anything. Her parents called the police. That's how I ended up here."

"I don't think I would waste my time and energy following my lady. That sounds crazy."

"Well, by the looks of things maybe you should have."

I was quickly learning that Johnny was by no means dumb, he had made his point three or four time since I had been here. Maybe Denise was seeing Rufus, I was so busy, I wouldn't have known it. Then Johnny told me he was on medicine for his nerves. That was when I felt guilty about telling him he was crazy for following his girlfriend, because he probably was. We sat talking for about another half an hour.

When it was time for bed that night, it was like the night before; sleep fled my eyes and when I did get to sleep, I was awakened, it seemed immediately, by a nightmare. I woke up shaking and sweating. All I could do was just lie there with my heart pounding in my bunk and wait for daylight.

The next day my mother and grandmother were there to see me. When I walked into the visiting area, my grandmother reached her arms to hug me. At first my mother just stood there, then she put her arms out. I gave her a hug, as she kissed me on the cheek.

"They told us we couldn't bring you any food," my grandmother said.

"So how are you feeling?"

"All right," I said, "I saw my lawyer earlier."

Mama was silent, Grandma did most of the talking. We talked about my lawyer and April of course, how she was getting ready for college. She told me Jimmy said hi and my friends J.C. and Rob asked about me. And how nice of a girl Denise was.

"They might let you go home till your pre-trial," she said.

I wasn't really thrilled about going home, I didn't want to go to a place where I'd be looking at my mother all the time, but I smiled anyway and looked as if I were happy about it. We talked for about twenty more minutes and Grandma said, "Baby, we got to be going now." We hugged and kissed. I watched Mama with a lump in my throat. I thought I saw her wipe the tears from her face as she turned around to leave.

The next couple days before I went before the magistrate, a man came to the detention center to talk to us about shaping up our lives and how not to become a career criminal as he had done. He talked about how when he was fifteen years old, he started selling drugs and how he began to use what he sold only a few years after he sold them. At first, he said, he was "king of the block," selling drugs to college kids and lawyers. He said then he began to use the drugs he sold after the dealer that supplied him threw a party. After that he began to rob and steal to support his drug habit and at the age of sixteen he was in juvenile detention for grand theft. He would shoplift expensive jewelry, then he got busted robbing a bank with a gun at the age of eighteen. He then mentioned if we had a drug problem then we needed to get help and that we didn't want to end up in prison. Then he continued with his story, after he got out of detention he looked for a job. He found one but he couldn't stay clean. He went back to the streets after he stopped going to work. His drug of choice said was heroin. "A heroin addict, gentlemen," he said, "cannot work.

"I had to rob and steal all day to get money to support my habit. I would stick up anyone," he said, "and I was only eighteen.

"If I knew your mother had money, I'd stick her up, even if you were my best friend. I didn't care," he said. "So what happened is that I stuck up the wrong person. I had to kill him to keep him from identifying me, but someone did see me. I got caught and here I am again, this time for life. I had to learn the error of my ways the hard way. I felt like nobody understood me because of my struggle. I hustled, out of greed. I wanted what I thought was the good life I drove the BMW, rode in the yachts, all those things at a young age, but like they say, all good things come to an end. My fast life took me to that speedy end. Pretty soon I was selling all my nice clothes. My effort was to get money anyway I could. If you want to be like me, keep doing what you're doing, if you don't want your freedom, if you want people telling you what to do, and confining you to a building not for hours, or months, or days, but for years. If you want to be locked up with people wanting to have sex with you 'cause they know they will never touch another woman again or they won't see a women for the next twenty years, keep doing what you're doing." Then he paused. "If you want to change and get a job, be grateful for what Creator gives you each day and forget greed. Jail is not worth the Cadillac, the diamond ring, or the nice clothes. If you're saying to yourself right now, 'It won't be me,' live a little longer, because I was standing where you are at one time, I was you. Right now, I'm clean. I go to AA meetings and I may not get out of jail till I get sixty, but I'm not going to let myself go. I found God in AA and it's all right today. I'm getting what I deserve and I can accept that today."

After Purcell Roberts left, we gathered into groups. I went into group C with six others. Mr. Hughes was our facilitator; he gave us all a piece of paper and a pencil then he asked us to write down three goals that we had for the future. The room was silent as everyone wrote on their pieces of paper. Then we gathered into a circle. Mr. Hughes went around the circle: the first two boys, Rafael and Maurice wanted to be millionaires. So Mr. Hughes asked what steps they were taking to reach their goal.

"Can you read?"

"I can read a little," Maurice said.

"Not that good," Rafael said.

"What type of jobs do you want?"

"Businessman where I can wear a suit every day," one person answered.

"Own my own business so I don't have to follow orders from no one," Maurice added.

"Okay, we have several people in here that want to own their own business. That's good, that's good," he said nodding his head, "What would you sell? Besides dope?"

The group laughed.

"You don't know, do you?"

Another boy held his hand up.

"Frank, go ahead."

"I want to go to college and become a sports newscaster. I want to be the next black Howard Coselle."

"What's keeping you from that goal?"

One boy's hand along with mine went up.

Mr. Hughes pointed to me.

"We're in here," I answered.

"Okay. Jail time. Let's talk about what got us here first and then we'll talk about making goals when we get out."

Rafael raised his hand. "It started when I started going with this girl."

"Uh-huh."

"Her parents were rich and I wanted to impress her, so I stole a fur coat, it was mink, and I gave it to her, then I began stealing expensive jewelry and selling it one day. I went back and stole some watches and I got busted and I got sent to detention for eight months. There I learned how to steal cars, so when I got out on parole, I started stealing cars and then I got caught. I was still on parole. Now I'm in here."

"So what are you going to do when you get out?"

"I'm not going home. I've got a girlfriend. I'll live with her."

"Why not home?"

"My father is on heroin and my mother is a prostitute."

"How do you know your mother is a prostitute?"

"She brings home men, one time one of the men wanted to sleep with me when I was eight years old. When I got old enough to be on my own, I joined a gang. Yeah, now my girlfriend takes care of me. I have no respect for my mother, because of what she did."

"How many of you feel like Rafael?"

More than half of the group raised their hands except for me and another boy.

"How many, if you had the chance, would go to a program to learn a skill, even if it's just to learn how to read, do math, to help get a good job when you got out?"

Hands flew up.

Then a boy name Maurice Howard spoke up. "I've been to a program that was supposed to do all that, but I can make more money sellin' dope. I mean, I got a family."

"So you're telling me you'd rather sell dope than to work a legitimate job?"

"Yeah."

"So if I were to call your girlfriend right now she would say Maurice takes care of me and my children, right?"

"Yeah." He smiled.

"Well, who's taking care of her while you're in here?"

"Welfare."

"Welfare? Do you pay child support?"

"Naw," Maurice said sliding back in his chair.

"Okay, so you said you had a family to support. Tell me how you support this family."

"I buy diapers and give her money when she needs it."

"You may be foolin' your girlfriend but you're not foolin' me. So let's say you get two thousand for sellin' dope and you give your girlfriend money for diapers so that comes to fifty dollars a month, maybe more, and—."

"No, I just give it to her like every once in a while."

"Once a month?" Mr. Hughes asked.

"Yeah, about that much."

"So you're saying you give your girlfriend ten dollars for diapers out of two thousand. Is that what you're telling me?"

"Yeah," he replied smiling.

"There is a point to this. So you give your girlfriend ten dollars a month and you give her money when she needs it? How often is that?"

"I don't know."

"Once a month or less than that?"

"Less than that," then he smiled again.

"So what do you do with all that money? You're livin' at home, you don't have a car, what do you do with it?"

"I go out, buy clothes."

"You do dope?"

"I get high a little here and there but I ain't hooked."

"A little here and there?"

"A little here and there, then that's it, man. I'm not a addict."

"How many of you in here do drugs? That includes alcohol."

All the hands went up including mine.

"How many of you might have a habit?"

Now this time three hands came up slowly.

"Look, man, I can handle my high." Maurice had sat up in his seat, the only person he had convinced was himself. "I don't care about comin' back in this joint," he said. "I'm going to make my money and if the police don't like it then I'll be back. Half of them get high anyway, you got your college boys and lawyers looking for a high, man, why not sell it?"

"Well, if you're locked up, who's going to be buying diapers for your baby?"

That's when he began to squirm in his seat.

"You come up in here, me and my tax dollars take care of the baby, you can't take care of your family if you're in here."

Maurice nodded.

"So the line about havin' to sell dope to support your family is a bunch of malarkey."

The group began to chuckle.

"Isn't it, Mr. Howard? Because if you care so much about this family you have, you'd be there now. And if you don't care about them, admit it. Find out why you don't care because if you know why you don't care, it might save you some trouble from coming in and out of here as if you were going through a revolving door."

"Man, you don't have to take it personal."

"Personal?" he laughed to himself. "You know what I take personal: when I see boys my kid's age in here because of denial, child abuse, and rape—kids with mental problems—murderers who kill just because 'he was talking to my lady at a party,' or 'he stepped on my foot and didn't apologize.' If you keep on at the rate your going...." He held up his hand as he paused. "The next step is an adult prison, not a detention home, your record will follow you wherever you go. So if you think I take it personal, yeah, I do. I see kids come in here like you all the time, in pain because of the conflict of how they think their life should be like and the reality of what it is actually like. Mr. Howard, as you may know, a junkie can be rich or poor. You know anyone on death row? That's reality, that's what I take personal." He looked at the clock and said, "Well boys, that's it, we're out of time. We'll talk about this tomorrow."

Chapter 5

I spent a week in the detention home when they decided at my pre-trial that because I would turn eighteen in a couple of weeks, they would try me as an adult. I was transferred to county prison were my bail was set. I was out of jail in three hours because the pastor of my grandmother's church put up bail for me. Jimmy and his wife Carol brought me home that day; there was dead silence in the car on the way home except for Jimmy, who tried his best to keep a lively conversation going. But it just wasn't the same. People were treating me so differently. Either they're too friendly or they distance themselves. My mother was ashamed of me. I could sense it.

When we arrived home, Jimmy said, "I'll stop by this Sunday and we can talk man to man."

"All right," I said.

I gave him five, closed the car door, leaving Mama still outside talking to Jimmy and his wife. April was in the kitchen with Grandma and when she saw me she ran over and rocked me in her arms and kept repeating, "Jerry, Jerry, I'm so glad to see you, I'm so glad you're at home." After she let me go, I noticed she was making chicken and dressing for dinner. "April, can you get the can of peaches out of the cabinet?" While she was getting the peaches, Mama came in the door. I excused myself to my room and told my grandmother to let me know when dinner was ready. When I got to my room, a frightening feeling came over me. My heart began racing, but I was trying to catch my breath. I felt as though a terrible secret had been exposed, the feeling was as if I were standing on a busy downtown street, with people whispering while they're looking at you strangely, and as you look down at yourself to see why, you notice you're naked. I decided then I would eat upstairs.

I was in my room when April called me for dinner, I went downstairs and got a plate and proceeded to fill it with food. I then announced to my mother that I was going to eat in my room. Mama just looked at my grandmother and nodded her head. I retreated to my room and closed the door. *I can't keep living like this*, I thought. I picked up the phone and called Denise.

"Hello, may I speak to Denise?"

"Just a minute," the voice said on the other end. I couldn't make out who it was.

"Hello?"

"Hey, what's up?" I said while getting comfortable on my bed.

"Where are you?"

"I'm at home," I said. I answered like a had everything under control. We talked for about a half hour, then she got quiet. "I got something to tell you but...."

"But what?" I hated when she started saying something and would hesitate to finish, so scared of everything.

"I'm pregnant."

"You're what?" I had to sit up from my comfortable position on the bed.

"I'm pregnant" she repeated.

"How do you know?" I asked her.

"I missed my period, so I went to the clinic to get a pregnancy test, and it came out positive." That's when I got angry, thinking, *Here I am, I'll probably go to jail and she's pregnant.*

"Well, you could have an abortion," I said. "What kind of life will this baby have if I'm in jail?" The next thing I know I thought I heard her crying, then all I heard was a dial tone; that's when I realized she had hung up on me. I was so scared, I went downstairs and told my mother what Denise had said.

After I told her she just looked at the floor shaking her head back and forth and saying, "Lord, this child's about to make me lose my mind." Then she looked up. "Where is she now?"

"At home."

"Her parents, do they know?"

"I don't know, Mama."

"I'm calling them. If they don't know, they will." I started to leave the kitchen and she said, "You just stay right here," and she left out the kitchen and I heard her saying, "I'm a talk to your grandmother and we're going to talk to her parents." I could hear her mumble, "I tell you, if it's not one thing it's another," as she went upstairs. I knew she and Grandma would have their conference. Ten minutes later they both came downstairs, questioning me, asking me how long had we been sexually active, and I told them two months when she told me she was pregnant over the telephone and hung up on me.

"Why did she hang up on you, Jeremiah?" Mama asked.

"I think because I told her she could have an abortion." My mother looked at me and rolled her eyes.

"You think you know so much, what's her number?"

"341-2020," I told her. She carefully pressed each number on the keypad. "Hello, is Mrs. Jones available; this is Mrs. Washington, Jeremiah's mother."

"Yes," then she looked up at me and shooed me away from the table.

"Excuse me?" she said she covered the receiver with one hand and mouthed *go upstairs* and pointed towards the living room, hinting for me to leave with her other hand. So I went up to my room and lay on my bed; that piece of chicken and dressing still lying on my bed was cold by now. I just set the plate on my dresser, trying to imagine what my mother and Denise's mother might be talking about. I stretched out on my bed, somehow I managed to fall asleep.

Chapter 6

When I woke up it was Saturday morning. I turned and looked at the clock. It was 9:30. I was happy because this meant Mama was at work. April, I hope, would be out. And Grandma would be home. I got up with the same clothes I had on the day before, and took the plate that I had on my dresser downstairs. When I saw my grandmother all dressed up I asked her, "Where are you going, Grandma?"

"I'm going to Bible class in a little while. What is that you have?"

"It's dinner from yesterday. I didn't eat it, I wasn't very hungry."

"The medicine, your father didn't like taking the medicine, that's why he died, he said it made him tired." I couldn't believe she was talking about him. After he died, they would never so much as mention his name around me or April.

"I'm just saying you've got a lot of your father in you," she said and then she smiled.

"When your mother and father got married, he was a good man. Your mother loved him."

"Mama's ashamed of me, isn't she, Grandma?"

"Your mama is still trying to take all this in. Baby, you know your father was bipolar, it wasn't easy for her, raising you and April and being married to your father. Maybe she feels as though she's reliving the past she lost her husband now she's losing her son." I understood.

"Your father killed himself, you know. He was an alcoholic and drug addict; he had mood swings, and wouldn't get help."

"Granny, I heard he went out with other women."

"Who told you that?"

"I overheard you and Mama talk about him at night when I was little and supposed to be asleep. You all were saying that there was a girl in the place with him the night he died, and then there was the one at the funeral." She looked up at the ceiling and sighed.

"Jeremiah, there were some things you and your sister were just too young to understand. It's true your father did sleep around with other women." I nodded my head.

"See, your father was too proud to get help from anybody. He wouldn't listen to your mother, his doctor, no one. I guess he felt as though the illness was some type of a weakness. He had to prove he was strong and when he was hurtin' he turned to hookers, wine and drugs and pushed everyone who ever tried to help him away. 'I can handle this myself' were his famous last words."

After all that, I began to think to myself, *No more drinking for me. I'm not goin' out like that.* I remember there were people there at the center who came and talked to us about drugs and alcohol. I remember what they said, too. Then my thoughts returned to our conversation. "Well, why didn't Mama just leave him then?"

"She wanted to, but by the time you and April were born, it just wasn't that easy, especially in those days. He would blame your mama for all his problems. He was a sick, sick man. I'm telling you this because I don't ever want you to end up like him."

Then I asked her about Denise. "Denise is fine, I'm sure of it, you just don't call her and don't go see her."

"Why not?" I asked.

"Because her parents don't want you to, that's why."

"Well, what's going to happen to the baby?"

"Jerry, you let your mother handle this right now," she said. "That night you came home drunk, you were lying, passed out on the front lawn. It took me, your mother and April to pick you up and carry you in the house and put you to bed. That night I prayed and I talked to Pastor Brown. We agreed a job might help you stay out of trouble."

"Grandma, those boys at school were jealous of me; they liked my girlfriend."

"You could have gotten a teacher or something."

"Grandma, everything was happening so fast, though."

"You shouldn't have hit him."

"But Grandma, I just knocked the knife out of his hand," I pleaded. "He could have killed me."

She looked at me and when I saw I had a audience, I told her, "The police beat me and then made me sign a statement confessing, saying I intentionally killed Rufus. I really didn't, I was just defending myself."

"Jeremiah?"

"What?"

"Did you tell your lawyer?"

"Yes, and she claimed that I gave the police a hard time and that they don't lie and I didn't have a case because I was a murderer and my credibility was no good."

"Look, I'm a tell you something," and she looked at me real stern and pointed. "Don't you repeat what you told me to anyone."

"But, Grandma, I'll go to jail," I wailed.

"Jeremiah, I'm old enough to have learned something in my lifetime. Just do as I tell you."

"Okay."

"Don't worry, now," she said as she hugged me and kissed me on my forehead. "Not even your mama, okay?" She smiled and hugged me again.

"Okay."

My grandmother has a way about herself, some call it a woman's intuition, some call it mother wit, whatever it is, I wanted to tell her about the knife, but for some reason or another, I think she already knew.

She walked to the living room. "I got to go to Bible class. Your mama will be here about six o'clock. Why don't you visit your friends?"

I said "okay" but I really didn't want to see them, but I decided to call them anyway. I called Rob first; he wasn't home; he was out somewhere.

"How are you, Jerry?" his mother asked.

"Fine, Mrs. Elliot."

"I'll tell him you called," and we hung up.

My mind then flooded with thoughts about Denise and everything that had occurred in the course of two weeks. I began to think about what Johnny said and I began to ask myself did she ever act strange. I went over in my mind how many times we had sex, when did she miss her period. I thought about signs that would tell me, maybe when she got pregnant. I wanted to call her, but no, I'd better listen to my grandmother on this one. But I could feel myself getting angry. Angry at this whole situation. I'll be the best father I can be. They won't catch me in some motel with some prostitute, that's for sure. That's the day I decided I really hated my father. I didn't want to be like him.

I pick up the phone and called J.C. He answered, "It's your dime," one of his favorite telephone greetings.

"What's up, man?"

"When they let you out, man?" He sounded excited.

"Yesterday," I told him.

"Man, we were wondering when you'd get out."

"I made bail." I didn't tell him Mama's church put up the money.

"You want to go out tonight? Celebrate?"

"No, can't drink, and besides I'm not in the partying mood. Denise is pregnant."

"Sure it's yours, partner?"

"I know it's mine, can't see her, though."

"No?"

"No, her parents won't let me."

"Francis is over here, she's mad 'cause I won't take her to the movies." I chuckled. "We went to the movies last week. I want to go out dancing she doesn't want to go, so I'm getting ready to take her home."

"All right, I'll talk to you later, man."

I hung up, laughing to myself. J.C. is a wannabe player. I think he considers it a weakness to admit he's in love, or maybe love has a different meaning for him. I remember one night we were drunk and arguing because he said he didn't like her. I told him, "If you don't like her, why are you always over her house? You've been with that girl since the seventh grade, man." I began laughing at him, saying, "Whenever you're with her, you're all over her, man." He tried to fight me that day. My thoughts returned to my father. *Well I'm going to marry Denise, if she says yes*, I decided. I knew what it was like growing up without a father and my child wouldn't grow up fatherless. The only thing that could complicate matters would be if I went to prison, which I knew I probably would do sometime. *She'll wait maybe.* I began to take off my clothes, deciding what I really needed was a shower. *I'll take a nap and catch up on my rest. I didn't sleep too well at the detention center, and maybe watch a little TV.* As I took my shower, I was busy planning out my future. Jeremiah Washington and Miss Denise Jones and my son, because I was going to have a boy. *I'll do my time, get out, find a job, and marry her*. I was thinking way ahead of myself. I thought I would talk to Jimmy see what he thought. I heard a knock at the door. I pulled my head out of the curtain and said, "I'm in the shower."

It was April. "Well hurry up, I got to go to the bathroom."

"Too bad," I yelled back. *Yep. Things are getting back to normal*, I thought as I smiled to myself.

Chapter 7

Mama, April and Grandma were already gone to church when I woke up the next morning, so I sat in the living room and watched some TV while I anxiously waited on Jimmy to stop by. I had plenty to talk about.

About an hour later they walked in the door. Mama, April and Grandma, all dressed up. Jimmy was right behind them.

"Missed you at service, man," he said as he wiped his feet on the floor mat.

"Yeah, I decided to stay at home."

"I understand." He was taking off his coat and hat.

"Come on in, Jimmy, and have a seat. Dinner will be ready in about an hour, so just make yourself at home," Mama was shouting from the kitchen. They idolized this man and I couldn't figure out why. It was as if only he could redeem my soul from hell, and I'd be saved. I quickly put it out my mind. I didn't believe it, I tried not to think about it.

"Watchin' the game?" he asked as he slapped me on my knee before he sat down.

"Yeah," I answered.

"We miss you at the job, Jerry. Maybe you could come back, you know, before it's time for the trial and everything."

"Okay," I said. "I'll be there tomorrow morning, You know they expelled me from school."

He didn't say anything but "um" and he had a stern look on his face when he said it. Then he pointed towards the TV saying, "Let's watch this game and eat dinner. We'll talk later."

"All right," I answered.

We watched the game, then soon it was time for dinner and we ate. Mama was busy telling Jimmy about Denise and me. And the fact that she was pregnant. And how keeping us apart wouldn't help the matter. But that she was going to respect what they say.

"I mean, it happened… and well, Jeremiah feels that since he might be going away, he wants her to have an abortion."

Jimmy looked at me and said, "Is that right?"

I was ashamed at first, but then I spoke up. "Well, at first I did, but I think that she wants to have the baby."

Mama interrupted. "But I know how my son feels and he doesn't need the responsibility," she explained.

"What about adoption?" Jimmy asked.

"Well, it's really up to Denise and what she wants to do," Mama answered.

"Doesn't anyone want to know what I want to do?" I blurted out.

Mama turned her head at me, rolled her eyes at me, giving me this look as if she couldn't believe I spoke. "Well what do you know, seeing as how you're only seventeen years old and about to go to jail for murder? You do realize that, don't you, or had you forgotten?"

"Calm down, Georgia," my Grandmother said.

"Calm down? He's sittin' there like he's got it all figured out. He's seventeen years old and don't know squat." Know I've seen my mother get upset before, but all of a sudden she burst into tears, excused herself, and ran upstairs. I thought about what Grandma said, her reliving the past.

The dinner table became quiet. I excused myself and pushed my plate to the side of table. I went to the living room and I heard Grandma and Jimmy talking quietly in the dining room as if they didn't want me to hear. So I sat staring at the television set, wondering when this evening was going to end. I needed someone to talk to, someone rational, someone who wouldn't fly off the handle so easily. So Jimmy came out of the dining room and said, "So what do you think?"

"What do you mean?" I asked.

"Back there while we were eating dinner, you said does anyone care about what you want? I'm asking you what do you want?"

"I… I want to marry her."

"Yeah?" he asked.

"If she'll wait for me. If I go to jail."

"You love her?"

"I don't know, but I know I care about her. I don't want my child growing up without a father."

"Yeah, well, that's good enough for me. I heard of people getting married for reasons less important than that."

"True," I said, "but I don't like the fact that they are keeping us apart."

"Well maybe it will give both enough time to think about your relationship. If it's meant to be, it will happen. But also respect her parents' decision. She's fifteen years old, scared, and her parents are probably upset. I mean, you two are just children. And you got to take into consideration you have murder charges hangin' over your head."

"Yeah." I understood that all too well. "I've been just waiting for the pre-trial, I guess."

"Worried?"

"A little," I said trying not to disclose too much. "But the truth of the matter is I need help… with alcohol." That wasn't the total problem but it was one of many, drinking was just a prelude. What really bothered me was to come later on in the conversation.

"My father was an alcoholic, I just thought I might be one, too."

"And that bothers you?" he said as if he didn't believe that was it. I was holding back and I think he detected it. So I continued.

"Yeah, it bothers me. I don't want to go that route, man. Like my father."

"How long have you been drinking?"

"Since I've been twelve."

"Well, Jerry, I know some boys a couple of years older than you that drank heavily, but they don't drink now."

"Yeah?"

"You want to meet them?"

I thought about it for a moment. "No, I'll just see if I can quit by myself."

"Your decision," he said.

"Jesus drank wine," I said defensively.

"Yeah, well, Jesus didn't lie passed out on his mother's front lawn, either."

"Oh, you heard about that?" I said.

"Yes I did."

Then I told him what really bugged me.

"You ever been in jail?"

"No never."

My first thought was, *He don't know what it's like to be afraid, I'm an outcast, he won't understand.*

"I worked with lots of kids, man, who have, boys who I consider to be just like my own kids," he said.

"Yeah." I smiled, that made me feel a little better.

"Really that's why I have that landscaping business to help boys like you stay out of trouble. They work for me and earn clean money. Gives them some hope." I noticed him looking at his watch. He stood up and said, "Well, Jerry, I'm going in the kitchen to say goodnight to your grandmother. I've got a wife and kids at home, you know." He bent down and shook my hand and said, "Don't worry about anything, and I mean it." He bent over and whispered in my ear, "I know what happened," he said and shook my hand again. I didn't say anything, I was dumbfounded, all I could do was watch as Jimmy went in the kitchen where my grandmother and April were sitting. I could hear him saying goodnight to my grandmother and April, and then telling my grandmother that he'd talk to her later.

"All right, Jimmy, feel free to stop by anytime," my grandmother yelled back.

"Thanks, Sister White, I'll do that." He put on his coat and hat and I opened the front door and he left out into the night.

All winter we plowed driveways and sidewalks. Mama kept talking about putting me in school. I told her I wasn't going. When she asked me why, I told her I just didn't want to. Secretly I didn't want that pressure. I really didn't want to hurt anyone else. She said she couldn't make me go, and as long as I was working it was fine.

Ever since that incident with Rufus, I hated school. I was tired, besides, I was embarrassed to be in the special classes where kids often made fun of us. I had to put up with it all while I was growing up. The memory of Rufus hung over me like a dark cloud, a constant reminder, but something wasn't right. I just knocked the knife out of his hand, how could I have killed him? I tried to shake the nervous feeling, but it came back; I forgot, someone reminded me. And it broke my heart every time I looked in my mother's face.

I hadn't heard from Denise and Mama hadn't heard from her parents. I guess I'd have to leave well enough alone. I stopped hanging around J.C. and Rob. We didn't have so much in common anymore. They were in school, I wasn't; they drank, I didn't. I'd see them occasionally at the store or round the neighborhood. I'd talk to them when I saw them, but life was taking a different turn for me. The way they were living, I understood the false perception that street life was glamorous. But I was searching for something more important. An inner peace. Something I felt Jimmy had; he had a wife, kids, he seemed like he was always happy, content. The fact that he listened to me made a difference. He seemed to try to see the world the way I did. He often said my world—which was the world of the teenager, and his world—the world of the adult, were separate, and he seemed to understand that. Then there was the feeling that there was just something about him. The feeling of peace I felt just being in his presence. I just couldn't figure how to have that myself.

Chapter 8

The day of the trial came. Mama and my grandmother were the only ones who attended. Jimmy had to work, so they sat watching and listening to the court proceedings. I was soon to understand the statement Johnny had made. I realized then the whole trial was a stage set before the world just to appear that justice had been served. I looked at my mother as they placed the cuffs on me. I put on that face I put on so many mornings when I was little. *Don't let it show*, I told myself. Mrs. Lipinski was no use at all; the prosecutor danced circles around her. She couldn't have been of less help if she hadn't bothered to show up. My grandmother looked heartbroken, my mother was isolated, they looked as if they were the only survivors deserted on an island after a shipwreck.

There's a double standard here, I thought to myself, and as they took me away I heard the prosecutor laugh. I walked away in anger thinking something was wrong. I was being blamed for something I didn't do. I knew it and I knew my grandmother knew it. My mother watching me, tears flowing uncontrollably down her face as they escorted me back to the jail cell where I would wait to go to the prison. They say count your blessings. I guess a little of Jimmy had worn off on me. I got life in prison and I wouldn't be due for parole until I was forty. I was sitting down, drowned in my thoughts when a man came up to me and called me by my name. I turned around and looked; there was a short white man standing in front of the cell with a big belly in a police uniform. "That was my sister's son you murdered. I have some advise for you while you're in prison. You better keep your nose clean as a whistle, boy, I'm going to be watching you."

"God knows what's happening," I said remembering my grandmother.

Then he glared at me up and down with his eyes and said, "There is no God for you, you worthless sneak. That's where all worthless murdering sneaks like you should be, locked up in prison," then he turned around.

I don't know what made me say it, but I yelled after him, "You're the sneak, you're the sneak." I watched him as he walked away out of the compound and down the dark corridor.

After that encounter, the parole officer came and asked if there were a problem. Of course I said no and continued to sit motionless in the cell while I waited for the officers to take me to Mansfield. We drove there and I sat with my wrist and ankles handcuffed, wondering to myself, *How did I manage to get into this?* I was racked with the torment of going to prison and maybe not getting out, *I might even die in there*, I thought.

Not a day went by since this had happened that Rufus didn't cross my mind. The way he looked when he got on that gurney. The way the police looked when they told me he died, how they beat me and got me to sign that statement, it was all coming back to me. I tried to rub the sweat forming on my forehead, but only the hard edge of my uniform scraped against my moist skin. *What does the future hold for me?* I wondered.

It was about a five-hour drive, and when I got to the prison it was nine o'clock. They sprayed me for bugs, I took a shower and got my uniform and toiletries. The guards led me to a cell. When I entered inside, my cell mate rose of the bunk and shook my hand.

"My name is Pat. What's yours?"

"Jeremiah." I had to quickly hold in the laugh because as I looked up there was no end to him. He looked more like a black sumo wrestler than an inmate.

"Jeremiah, you can take the top bunk the bottom is mine. You smoke?"

"No."

"Drink coffee?"

"No."

"Don't start. You'll have an easier time in here. Sit down and make up your bunk and watch some TV with me; ain't nothin' to do." I sat down and began making up my bunk. He seemed pretty cool. I had to hold in my laughter; I couldn't get over thinking about Pat. I don't think he was gay, but maybe the name was just a test. I mean, you wouldn't go up to him and say "hi Patricia" or anything like that. He must weigh 300 pounds easy, maybe more. I sat and watched him eat a bag of chips while watching the news as I made up my bunk and sat on it, careful not to hang my feet down over around his head.

"Where are you from?" he asked.

"Cleveland."

"Hm. I'm from Akron. I had a woman. I let her go, though, no sense in her waiting around for an old man to get out of prison. I got three kids that come to see me least once a month. They brought me this TV. You got a woman?"

"Yes," I said in pride. "She's expecting our child."

"How much time you got?"

"Life."

"You a bango?"

"A what?"

"A bango, you know, someone who likes to fight."

"No, I'm not hardly a bango."

"You'll make parole," he said confidently.

"Lights out," I could hear the guard yelling.

"Well it's time to hit the sack." He turned off his TV and lay in his bunk. His cell looked like a miniature apartment; plants, cookies, and bags of chips lying around a small TV set with a radio attached. I lay down in wonder and for the first time in months I fell right to sleep.

The next few months weren't hard, to tell you the truth; it was like another world in there. A trickle down effect to the ghettos, which was made up of people that had been carved out and left as the product of an unmerciful pious society. A people left to itself where the murderer was king, the thief was considered as high a status as a well-paid businessman, and the pimp was admired by all. Well, it wasn't long before I was approached by two men while I was on the way to the laundry room who I think were gay; they told me I had pretty eyes. I proceeded to the laundry room and then they stopped me again; this time they asked did I need a girlfriend to make my time in here tolerable. I gave them my solemn answer, "No." I was to afraid they were speaking about themselves. I told Pat what they said later on that evening. Pat confirmed my beliefs that they were talking about themselves. He also told me they prey on men that give them cigarettes and coffee, some of the officers and lawyers bring them drugs. They do anything they can get their hands on.

"Do they have AA meetings in here?" I asked since I didn't hear anyone mention them.

"Tomorrow you can ask Shortie; he's the short, stocky, bald-headed guard. He will tell you what time they start."

"Do you go?"

"No, I never had a problem with drinking or drugs. My problem was with the women I fooled around with."

"Why are you here?" I asked him.

"Because of a woman I met in St. Louis named Rena. She wasn't my old lady, just a girl I was foolin' around with while I was running drugs from Mexico. I was involved in a drug ring until I got busted. Rena turned out to be a FBI agent. I'd have her ride with me to Mexico, she'd pick up the package, meet me at the airport in Arizona, then drive to St. Louis. It went smooth for a while until they raided the dope house. I heard them as they knocked down the door. I didn't know what was happening; I was in bed when all of a sudden I was surrounded by police. I was relieved it was the police, because there's people running around robbin' dope houses and killin' people and taking their drugs and money. After I was set up, and sent up, she disappeared as quickly as I met her." I listened as I sat on my bunk watching a rerun of Bonanza. That became a regular pastime. Pat just finished eating his third bag of pretzels.

I wrote my grandmother and sister, telling them of my life here in the prison. I became used to the prison. We worked while we were in there; some worked in the cafeteria, some worked in the library, I worked in laundry. I decided to spend some of my time getting my GED. Even though I wasn't getting out till I was sixty, I still might go to college; at least that's what my sister told me to do in her letters. Besides, she said I had to stay positive and keep busy. At night I would lie awake thinking about the trial. Maybe the truth will come out one day. And for the first time in a long time, I felt alone. So I was sitting there in the cell, looking at the ceiling. I didn't have money to hire a decent lawyer. And yet I felt that was part of the plan. I did hit Rufus with that chair. He was so high, but they never brought that up in court. I hadn't felt this way since my father was alive. So I did what I would do when he was alive, he beat my mother and I felt alone, not being big enough to help her. I prayed and told God to help her and I believe God heard me. Maybe that's why my dad died. I'm older now, even and I might not get an answer, because I don't read the Bible too much, I don't go to church, but what I do know is he is just and he knows what's going on and I believe if he does exist, he might help even me.

I'd become good friends with Pat and I hadn't been here for a week. It was time for lunch and I looked and I saw a familiar face, a fellow I knew from the neighborhood. I walked up to him and spoke. "What's up, Junior? Jerry, you remember me."

"What up, Jerry?" He took me hand and shook it. "Yeah, I remember you, you lived over there on Way and you hang out with J.C and Rob."

"Yeah."

"What you doin' in here, man?"

"I got in a fight at school." I didn't go into too much detail. His eyes lit up.

"A fight, man? You what, seventeen?"

"Eighteen. Dude died on the way to the hospital." I only confessed because I knew he would know I wouldn't be in here for just a fight.

"Yeah, I think I heard about that, man. You know my cousin Tony? He's a tall, light-skinned fellow, drives a yellow Buick."

"Yeah, I know him."

"He told me someone killed Rufus, except he wasn't quite sure who did it, you know, there were a lot of rumors going around."

"Yeah," thinking I could testify to that. I remember hearing some of those rumors myself.

"I didn't like him, man," Junior stated. "He started some stuff with my cousin and his friends, he always would shoot off his mouth and act like he was going to do something, flashing knives and guns on people. Rufus was crazy; a lot of people didn't like him."

"Yeah," remembering the police and what my grandmother told me. "Rumor had it he liked Denise, my girlfriend," I added.

"He was that type, man."

"They didn't even bring that up at all. I had a job, car and everything. He was jealous. That trial. I don't want to talk about it."

"Right, well, his uncle's a cop."

"Yeah," I continued, "so my lawyer asked me did I want to appeal."

"I tell you somethin' about lawyers," Junior added, "especially if you have one appointed by the court. You might as well be standing there defending yourself."

I saw that Junior was a lot like Johnny; he may not be an authority on the subject, but he made a bitter point. Changing the subject, I asked him, "Why are you here?"

"I was robbin' people's houses, tryin' to make some money. I'm getting out in a couple of years, goin' down south to live with my aunt." I nodded my head. I didn't know that he was into stuff like that, now if I remember correctly, Junior was about five years older than me; his cousin was my age. We talked for a while, I told him I was planning to go to some AA meetings, he mentioned that he went, and if things worked out right he wouldn't be back. We talked about Rufus, women, and drinking.

"Yeah," I said looking down at the ground, "I won't get out till I'm sixty."

"We shouldn't be here," Junior preached. "We should be in college, man, or have a job or somethin', not this, not here, man. This is my second time here. I got out the first time and got right back messed up on that dope, started fooling with the same crowd I was messin' with before I came. Next thing you know, I'm back here. When I leave I ain't coming back." By the look on his face, I could tell he'd probably come back. We talked about fifteen minutes more; I felt bad for Junior because he was right, we shouldn't be there. The conversation ended as we both had to leave the dining hall to go on to our separate units.

The mail is passed out in the morning. I waited to hear my name; when he called me I went to get my letter; it was from my grandmother. After I read the letter, I put it down and sat on my bunk. I felt relieved, hearing from my grandmother and after being here a month, I decided to call Rob and J.C. During our personal time we can go to rec, or gym or we can use the time to make phone calls.

First I called Rob, but they wouldn't accept the charges (we had to call collect), so I assumed that he was not at home. I called J.C. His mother accepted the charges. He was there so we talked for a while. He also talked about how he and Rob were out and how Rob got a ticket for driving under the influence. We exchanged stories; I was telling him about how things were in here, and then he gave me the scoop on Denise. "Denise told Rob that Rufus approached her about a week before the fight saying that he wanted to get back together with her. She told him she already had a boyfriend, so he told her he was going to wipe you off the map. Now you hear Annette, her cousin, tellin' everybody Denise is in Texas with her aunt."

I started to tell J.C. what I thought, then I heard my grandma's words echo in my head. I decided the less I said about it the better. I ended my conversation with him and hung up.

I didn't think about Denise much that day, but the next day I called my mother and asked her why she didn't tell me that Denise was in Texas, and whether or not she had the baby. She didn't think that I needed to worry about that right now. So I hung up the phone angry, but later I calmed down.

A couple days had passed. Mama and my grandmother came down to see me. When I went to greet them they had a solemn look to their faces. I laughed and said, "You two look as if someone died. They both look at each other and my grandmother said, "You better sit down, Jerry," so we all sat down. "Your mother has something to say."

"Jerry, Rob and J.C. are no longer with us."

I said, "What do you mean?"

"I mean they're dead, Jerry."

"What happened? Do you know?"

"Jerry, all I know is that they had been drinking and then went head on into traffic and crashed into a truck. They died instantly. It was horrible."

I shook my head in disbelief, thinking, *I just talked to J.C. not even a week ago.*

"Well they were on their way to pick up J.C.'s girlfriend and they never made it. It was all in the papers and the news."

"When are the funerals?"

"I don't know yet. But I will get you the obituaries."

My grandmother held my hand from across the table. "I'm sorry, Jerry."

"Thank you for coming way down here to tell me. When did all this happen?" I asked her.

"The same night you called asking about Denise." I thought to myself, *This can't be happening.* "I just talked to J.C., Ma, and he told me that Rob got a ticket for driving under the influence."

"Just be grateful, baby, you weren't with them," Mama said.

My grandmother nodded, talked for a while, and then they had to be going. She assured me Denise was okay, and we exchanged hugs and they left. I went back to my unit. They were like brothers to me. I wondered about what Mama said, "Just be grateful you weren't with them." I thought to myself, *Why wasn't I with them?* Maybe God was watching over me after all.

Chapter 9

Several months passed by since Rob and J.C.'s deaths. July 2 rolled around; it was the day of the birth of my daughter. Denise wrote me a letter and sent a picture with the letter; her name was Jasmine Jones. Denise asked me not to tell my mother she wrote me because after the trial her parents didn't think it was good she see me, and they moved her down south where they thought I would not know where she or the baby was. Well, her parents had succeeded where I would not be able to see my daughter, but Denise promised me she would send me pictures even though she might not write that often. She still cared about me, she said, and hoped her parents would change their mind, if they didn't then she hoped I'd understand. She'd never forget me; she would tell Jasmine about me. "They can't keep her from you when she gets older, right?" I silently agreed as I read. Then I began writing Denise back, in secret. I'd sign my letters "W.J." so that her aunt would not know who was sending her letters. She found out anyway from the postmark and confronted her. When Denise wrote me, she told me she didn't mind; she wasn't going to report it to her parents. It was her business who she wanted to be with.

I concealed the letters she wrote secretly inside of my mattress near the bottom. When Denise wrote her letters, it seemed as though I might expect a visit from her. I don't know if I did it out of insanity, but I began telling her that I was getting an appeal and I'd be coming home. Every time I ended my letter, I'd say "see you soon," promising her we would be a family. When the truth was I probably wouldn't see my child until when she grew up or unless

Denise let her visit me in prison; anyway I continued to write these ridiculous letters hoping the fantasy would come true. I hoped that it would keep her happy and optimistic. I realized these were selfish motives and that I would have to tell her the truth. So I wrote her a letter and told her that there was no appeal and I didn't want to lose her, and that if she wanted to she could wait, if she didn't mind marrying me when we would become older.

I was feeling pretty good about the fact I told Denise the truth, and despite my fears, sent the letter later on that evening. I got into my first fight there at the prison. By the time they broke it up, I had the boy on the floor where I had almost began to kick him in the face. I stopped myself before I did it. The security guard Shortie asked me what happened. When I told him, he said they had to put us both in isolation. So I was there for about three days, and the only lesson I learned from being there is that either you die letting someone beat you to death, or you fight back and go in isolation. It didn't sound like a reasonable payoff, but more like an irrational solution to a problem without an justifiable answer.

But as soon as I came out, Jimmy was there to see me. "What's up, brother?" chanting his usual phrase, smiling. I almost thought he knew what happened. I lowered my head.

"I got in a fight."

"I can't hear you. You got what?" he held his hand cupped to his ear.

I guess I was mumbling a bit. I know he heard me, but I cleared my throat anyway and repeated, "I... got into a fight."

"You want to talk about it?"

"Yeah," I said.

"Tell me what happened." Then Jimmy leaned back into his chair and looked directly into my eyes with a solemn look on his face.

"Well," I began to explain, "I was sitting watching TV and this big dude, he came up to me and tells me I'm sitting in his seat. So I said, 'Man there four other chairs around here; can't you sit in one of those?' That's when he started talkin' about, 'Naw, man, this is my chair, man,' and all this. I still wouldn't get up, so he grabbed me and that's how it started."

"You get hurt?"

"Not much, a bruise on my arm from him twisting it."

Jimmy shook his head and began to tell me a story. "When I was little, I lived off of Scoville. There was this family nobody bothered 'cause there were thirteen of them and if you fought one you had to fight them all. When I was in elementary they called me Fast-foot Jimmy." He smiled and laughed.

ANGELS ONLY STAND
WHERE CHERUBIM TAKE FLIGHT

"There was this bully name Bernard in our neighborhood. I was always little; I couldn't fight, but I could run. One day he approached me threatening to beat me up. I took off as fast as I could down the street and I ran in the house looking out the living room front window for Bernard. So here he comes, four to five minutes later, huffing and puffing, calling me names on our front lawn. This went on for about a week until one day my mother yelled and told him if he didn't leave she'd call the police. He left me alone after that. Growing up in that neighborhood was a lot like fighting in WWII." Then a stern look fell upon his face as quickly as the smile had left. "Be careful," he said. "You're like a son to me; I don't want anything to happen to you." I smiled on the inside, relieved to have someone I could consider a father figure; it really meant a lot to me.

"You know they tease me; call me Ali now."

"Yeah, it may be fun now, but you may have to defend that title again."

I nodded, understanding what he meant. "I'll be careful." I knew by the way Jimmy checked his watch it was time for him to go. He put his hat on and shook my hand.

"Call me if you need anything," he said. "Even if you just want to shoot the breeze or need some money on your books, man." I saw him off. He was like my father, the father I never had. When he left, I had a lump in my throat, tears were forming in my eyes, but I held them back. When he was gone I went back to my unit.

I attended school here at the prison. Along with getting my GED, I was also in a car mechanics class. Two days after Jimmy visited I had the pleasure of meeting who would be one of my best friends while I was here at the prison. I was standing outside when I felt someone close behind me.

"Jerry, right?" I looked and saw this short white fellow standing next to me.

"Yeah," I said.

"Man, I've been watchin' you; you're an all right dude. You seem to got your head to together." I was surprised, at first at his language; he was white, but he sounded black.

"Yeah," I answered him. I was watching him, too, because he had a cigarette in his hand and while he talked he pointed at me with the end of his cigarette; his head was kind of cocked to the side.

"I thought you handled yourself like a champ the other day; no wonder they call you Ali. Man, I saw the whole thing. You go to those AA meetings?"

I turned around and looked at him and said, "Yeah, I go."

"What are they like? I never been to one."

"They're all right, gives you something to do, something to think about."

"I was thinking about going myself, I just didn't know anyone who went."

I nodded and said, "My father died, killed himself. He was an alcoholic and drug addict. I told myself I'm not goin' out like that. I'm a make some changes in my life, the way I've been living." I soon found out that his name was Scott; like I had said before we became good friends we went to meetings together. He seemed pretty cool; we got along pretty well. As we got to know each other, he began to tell me these stories.

One day we were talking and he all of a sudden began to tell me why he was there. "I stole cars," he said. "I'd sell the parts. I even owned a car made up of stolen parts which when I brought it home, my mother had a fit. She asked me where did I get money to buy a car, she asked." He was looking up smiling at this point. "I just told her that my woman bought it for me. I was messin' with this woman; she was twenty-five years old, man. I mean, I'm seventeen years old and she's diggin' me and I got caught up with everything and boom, I ended up here." What he failed to tell me was that he was a addict. I could tell by the track marks up and down his arms, which was probably why he stole cars.

I blurted out, "Well, you got to trust in God." I didn't know what else to say. I wasn't an authority on God, but I still felt as though I had to give this sermon. "It's not fate that we are here, I mean, we did things that we regret, but my boys back home, man, died in a car accident. They were drunk, man. I wonder sometime why it couldn't have been me. The funny thing about it is, I talked to them the day it happened."

Me and Scott talked for a while and some of his friends came around we all started talkin' and jokin' around and things. Soon it was time to go in.

They reassured me if there was anything I needed I could come to them. They seemed to like me; most of them had encountered the same thing. They didn't like the boy that I fought and who he hung out with. Anyway, that's how I got involved in this clique. Some were in prison for murder, and stealing. They became my friends. They helped me out and looked out for me at the prison, making sure no one else bothered me.

Three months went by, I hadn't heard from Denise but I still wrote her more regularly. *Everything's going to be fine*, I told myself, *maybe her aunt is keeping her away from writing*. I kept writing, telling her of my dreams. When I got out I would go to Texas and get her. I know it was hard for her raising Jasmine by herself and all. I felt guilty because in my mind I'd promised myself I would always take care of her and the baby.

Scott and I would get together, swapping stories about our girlfriends and how we ended up in here, what our plans were when we would be released. He confessed to his drug problem; it was just as I expected, he was a heroin addict. When he told me, I told him I had suspected it and pointed to his arm. He didn't seem surprised. I asked him when it stopped being for fun. Stealing the cars. He began a story. "I was fifteen when I first started using heroin. First it was fun, all up until I graduated from college. I got a job and couldn't hold it down, mainly because of my drug abuse. Finally I began to steal cars and sell the parts as a way to support my drug habit. I couldn't stop using and I couldn't stop stealing; that's when I ended up here.

That's when I learned a lot of the boys here had a lot of problems with drug addiction at a young age and the sad part is they grow up and had to either rob or conduct some illegal activity just to feed their addiction. Others had mental illness, and abuse issues from their youth that manifested in their puberty, such as rape and other problems that aided in their delinquency. A lot of us looked up to Shortie and saw him as what you would call a mentor, because he was a lot older than most of the men here.

It was going on eighteen months and it was a Friday and I was going to play a game of pool. When I entered the rec center I spoke to the guard they called Mr. Jingling; they called him that because you could here him coming by the jingling of his keys. Then I sat down with a couple of men. We were laughing and joking around until this fellow walked up to me, he's about five-eight, and asks me why I was there. I told him because I was waiting to play winners. Then three others walked up and kind of pinned me to the wall. The security guard closed the door to the room and lit up a cigarette and smoked it as one of the boys said, "No, we want to know why you're here at the prison."

Well by that time I was nervous and I was outnumbered and the guard just smiled. So I told him that I was there because I got into a fight and the boy died on the way to the hospital. Then he puffed his cigarette and said, "Hey… my uncle says you're a worthless sneak."

I said, "What?"

"My uncle said you're a worthless sneak," he repeated.

"Your uncle, right. I guess he's my uncle, too," I answered.

The smile came off his face and he put his cigarette out on the floor, then he grabbed me.

"That was my cousin you killed."

I thought, *This cannot be happening*. The next thing I know I was lying on the ground in a fetal position as six white boys continued to beat me. I placed my arms around my head and drew my elbows to my chest to keep them from kicking my face and beating on my chest. Someone stomped on my side and kicked me in the back. They were beating my so bad all I could do was lie there and take my beating like a man. I heard someone say, "He's dead, he's dead." I lay there until I heard a voice.

"Jerry." Someone shook me. "Jerry."

I rolled over to see him and I began spitting up blood; that is the last thing I remember.

When I came to, I was in a hospital room. The doctor told me when I woke that they almost killed me if it weren't for Shortie, one of the guards who I had gotten to know there at the prison. They rushed me to the hospital. I had two cracked ribs, a broken jaw, a shattered knee and a slight concussion. I was to spend the next couple of months in the hospital until I could walk on my own again. I wrote my grandmother telling her I believed someone was trying to kill me in here and I was scared that I didn't think I would make it out of prison alive. I told her this was not a delusion. When she wrote me back and said:

Dear Jeremiah,

I received your letter. I don't want you to worry. I believe God has a special angel guarding over you, praying for you, because I asked God to do that for you. I believe he will get you through. Lately, I have not been feeling well, and even though your mama may have not told you, I'm very sick. Jeremiah, no matter what people say, I will always believe in you. I still remember when your mother brought you home and I held you as small as you were, wrapped in that little blanket. I still wish I could hold you once more and comfort all your fears. But you are still and always will be my grandson, my baby.

Love,

Your Grandmother

ANGELS ONLY STAND
WHERE CHERUBIM TAKE FLIGHT

When I read the letter, I was worried about my grandmother. No one told me she was sick. I guess Mama didn't want me to worry. I put the letter away and went to talk to Shortie. We were talking about the fight I got into. "They could have killed you," Shortie said. "You know everyone makes mistakes, man. Nobody grows up and says 'I want to be a stick-up kid, I want to stick people up to support my dope habit.' It just don't happen that way. Poor people can't buy dope, man. Some of these men will never be able to live outside these walls. I see you, you'll go somewhere in life. If they don't give you a hard time in here you'll make parole. It's hard doin' time; I could tell you some real horror stories." I thought about what Shortie said. I didn't have any more problems from those boys or from the security guard; after the incident he miraculously quit his job. I was soon back hanging out with Leonard and my other friends. They asked me how I was and they told me that if I had problems from them again to let them know. I told them it was okay. I didn't want to start any commotion in here, but I knew that Shortie and Pat were watching my back also. They understood. I was feeling stronger as I worked out in the weight room every day.

It was a Saturday, they were passing out mail, and I received a letter from Browning, Texas. Even though I hadn't heard from her in a while, I knew it must be from Denise. I smiled, stuck out my chest and proceeded to my cot where I could have some privacy while I read this letter. My thoughts danced to the hope of just hearing from her again. I read the letter and to my surprise she wanted the relationship to end and she didn't want to take care of the baby. I was so angry, but why; after I had lied to her for so long, it was only to be expected. What woman was going to wait for a man who wouldn't get out of prison until he was sixty? I must have been crazy to even think she would go for something that stupid, or maybe I mistook her for a fool. I took the letter and tore it up in so many pieces until no one would be able to read it. No one was going to find this letter and throw it up in my face. When we had our free time, I called Mama.

"Mama, you know Denise wrote me this letter," I explained to her. "Have you talk to her parents?"

"No baby, I haven't."

"Well, Ma, listen to this: she doesn't want the baby. She says I'm in jail and I'll never amount to anything and that she's going to marry some man down there."

"Well, Jerry, this is the first I've heard of this, where the letter come from?"

"Browning, Texas," I told her.

"Well I'll call her parents later to see what's going on." After we hung up, I was angry. I wanted so badly to break out of this place and if I could have found a way I would have. A week later, luckily for me, Jimmy came to visit.

"What's up, Jimmy?" I shook his hand.

"You brother. You. You're lookin' good." We both chuckled a bit and sat down.

"What's new? How are you feeling?" he said looking me dead in my eyes, looking at me as if he knew I would break down. Since I knew he might know Denise was involved with another man, and I wasn't feeling so cheerful, instead of lying I may as well cut right to the point.

"Did Mama tell you about Denise?" Since I knew she told him everything anyway.

"Yes, she told me. I also hear that your daughter is coming here to Cleveland. Your mama is going to take care of her here. Isn't that good news?" He seemed to be so happy.

"How do you know?" I asked him.

"I talked to your mama last night. I told her I'd come out and give you the good news." I looked at him, but I didn't share his joy. He stopped grinning and looked at me and said, "Look, Jerry, she's on drugs. Her aunt can't take it anymore. Denise is with some man three years older than her. There's just not much that they can do with her anymore."

"And Jasmine is coming here?"

"Yes."

"When?" I asked.

"In a couple of weeks. Look, Jerry, your mother asked me to come out here to tell you 'cause she just couldn't make it out." I nodded my head, understanding, but that wasn't quite the problem. "There will be other girls, Jerry. When you get out, the world will be different, you'll see." But that was the problem. I got by in here thinking of Denise, thinking of a maybe having a future with her and now, nothing.

"How is Mama picking up Jasmine?" Since I knew she didn't have a car.

"Denise's parents are bringing her here. Before you called they were planning on putting the baby in foster care or placing her up for adoption. But your mama insisted she stay with her. So they agreed that Jasmine should live with her."

By the time Jimmy left, I'd plummeted to an all time low. Call me weak, but I died inside the minute Jimmy left. Things became overwhelming; the stress was just too much. Daily I'd gather my friends around for the "poor me" sermon. Finally they told me to get over it. "There's plenty fish in the sea." I knew that, but the hard part wasn't catching the fish, it was finding the one I really liked. I became totally withdrawn. I wasn't working out. I sat in front of the television set and no one seemed to bother me. I wasn't getting over it. I couldn't sleep. I couldn't eat.

About a month after that, I was watching TV when the guard said I had visitors. I went to the visitation room; there were Jimmy and my mother. I hugged my mother and Jimmy and sat down. My mother began to talk. "Your grandmother died; the funeral was yesterday. We thought it was best to tell you after the funeral...." I stared at Jimmy and looked back at my mother; her lips were moving as she periodically looked at Jimmy and then me. At that point I had tuned everything out. Mama's lips moved with no sound coming out and my sorrow was so great I didn't feel. I cried mostly through that visit. I didn't care who saw me. When she finished delivering her speech, I stood, staring off, careful not to look in her eyes. She placed her hands on my shoulders and kissed me on my left cheek which was wet with tears. After my mother stood off to the side waiting with her head down while I reassured Jimmy that I would be okay, he shook my hand and caught up with her and then they left.

I was standing outside with Pat as we were talking to one of his friends that I had met. He and one of his friends owned an after hours joint and he was serving time in jail for soliciting women. He was talking and cursing at the same time.

"Hey, watch your language," I told him.

"Man, I don't see no women up in here, do I?"

"No, it's just something I was brought up with. My grandmother...."

"Yeah, it's cool though, you got the virgin ears and all that."

"Yeah."

"It's all right." He held out his fist and I took my fist and lightly tapped it on top of his; this was a symbol of friendship and peace. After that he continued, "But look here, man, I gettin' ready to call one of my women. When she gits paid, I gits paid." He began to walk away in a crazed shuffle with his hands in the air, shouting back saying, "You understand, it ain't nothin' but a thang, they can't keep a brother down, I still got my money and my women."

Pat began to laugh. Junior made the comment about how he has all these women. "I don't see how he has all those women. The one that was here the other day, man, you should have seen her. You talk about the Commodores, a brick house? She was built." He held out his hands as he spoke. He made an outline of the shape of a woman's body. "I mean curves was everywhere, man." He added, "And they even know the brother's in jail and he ain't gettin' out anytime soon, my lady." He said, "Soon as I told her I was in prison, left me."

"Mine left me too, man," I added.

"Hey," Pat said, "the brother's got game, man. He's a pimp by trade."

"What do you mean by that, Pat?" I asked.

Pat took his hands and rubbed them together, then he began to explain. "Well, little brother, seeing as how you got the virgin ears and all, but what I mean by that is, let's see how I can put this...." Pat rubbed his hands together and said, "That's what the brother does best."

"Yeah, well it ain't in me, to pimp no women like that," I said.

Junior echoed, "Ain't in me neither, man."

"Well now, that's how the brother survives," Pat explained.

Pat walked away it was almost time to go in. I was staring off into space thinking about Lucky, that's what they called him, because he had his way with women. He had a television set, radios, all sorts of food and cigarettes, and magazines; his women gave the brother everything. The woman he was calling was a lawyer who was handling his case; rumor had it that she put money on his books and passed him drugs when she came to visit. I even think he had sex with her in here. Anyway he would get naked pictures of his girlfriends and barter them here inside the jail for cigarettes, food, and coffee.

And for a moment I caught myself envying him, wishing I could be like him, but deep down inside I knew I wasn't that type of person. I didn't have it in me to make girls do stuff like that and I knew I had to accept that.

I was still in a thinker's daydream. I didn't notice Scott approaching me. "What's up, man?" he asked. I watched him as he brushed the ground with his feet.

"Any way to get out of here?" I asked him.

"You don't want to do that," he answered.

"No?"

"No, just give the police or guards another reason to hunt you down and put a bullet in your back while you got your back turned. Another statistic, another black man dead."

"Yeah, I guess you're right."

"Want a cigarette?"

ANGELS ONLY STAND
WHERE CHERUBIM TAKE FLIGHT

"No, I plan on walking out of this place when I turn sixty. No pine box for me." I patted my hands on my chest. "I'll be healthy."

"Yeah, well my uncle drank and smoked and he lived to be ninety."

"Well I should live to be a hundred then."

"Wanna box later on? You can get out some of that frustration."

"That sounds like a plan. I can do that." I put a smile on my face even though I didn't feel up to doing anything. I decided to pretend to be happy when I was around my friends.

I met Scott at the gym where all the convicts went to pump iron. The bigger the build, the less likelihood of someone starting a fight with you, because what you bench press determined whether you won the fight or not.

Anyway, I saw Scott smoking his cigarette. When he saw me he butted the cigarette and greeted me.

"Hey, Jerry."

"What's up, Scott?"

"Didn't think you'd make it."

"Yeah, truth is I almost didn't."

"Let's do the press," he said.

"Okay. How much can you lift?" I asked.

"175."

"Okay." I told him at the press, "Let's start with 100 and go up."

"Okay."

I added twenty-five pounds gradually, so in the end he was pressing 175, then we switched places.

"Okay," he said. "How much?"

"190, but not all at once. I work up to that."

So he had me press 125 first, then gradually added 25 pounds until I got up to 175, then he took off the two twenty-fives and added on fifty, then he added twenty, then five. We both took turns three times. I placed the weight down and then we went over to the punching bag. We took turns spotting each other, first he'd spot and then me. I was covered with sweat when I left the gym, so I went to the shower, the only place in the whole prison I don't particularly like to be. Fights started in the shower and newcomers that looked soft would have their masculinity tested in the shower. It must have been the fact that I was doing time for murder, and people thought that I was crazy, and saw that I could stand my ground; they usually left me alone. The ones that fought back were usually accepted into the prison. The ones that didn't, days were spent here in slavery. The inmates had a good time telling you what to do, taking your snacks and anything else they wanted. But there were always a couple of people that always had to test your manhood. This particular day I was standing in the shower and a man made a comment. "I bet if I had a piece of that you'd be all right."

I guess news of me and Denise had spread quickly, so I walked over and said, "A piece of what, man?" and I punched him in the mouth before he could answer. After that, I noticed his mouth was bleeding and he began to back up. "A piece of what?" I said. I stood with my fist. I started to hit him again, but I noticed he retreated with his hands covering mouth; it was bleeding, so I restrained myself and I walked out of the shower room and put on my uniform. I realized sometimes you have to stand up for yourself. I didn't want to have hit him, but if I hadn't he might try me another time. I had no other option than to fight. The language some people only understood was the mighty fist.

Chapter 10

Pat wasn't in the cell when I went to lie down after that encounter. I went there to think about things and to wonder if I were in for a confrontation. Jimmy hadn't come. It'd been almost a month since I'd seen him. I began thinking about the way life was. I did believe there was a God. Jimmy gave me a Bible that I had begun to read after my grandmother died. I went to church once here at the prison but didn't really feel comfortable. I felt isolated from the world, being a African-American male was not easy. I heard people say in prison that the government threw drugs in black communities, hoping to wipe out our people or to make us drug dependant so we could not function as a people or as individuals, we would always be on the bottom, by killing each other. What was it about us that people feel this distinct hatred? I wondered about the things my grandmother used to talk about. I think she must be thinking of me in heaven then. I know she's looking down on me, praying for me, and I believed God had one of his angels looking after me, just like she told me. The rest of the week went by fine. I was finally coming out of the depressed mood I was in and I actually began to feel better. I still feel like something spiritual happened as I pondered about life that week. What it meant to be black and how it fit spirituality in the scheme of things. My total being in the midst of the universe and what was my place in it. What did these thoughts mean? I knew I could make the space in my world better by changing my attitude.

I was afraid, but I began to pray that night. It was the first time since I had been little. I told God that if he got me out of here, I promised to help anyone that needed it, if he gave me the means to do so. That's how I had found my oasis, helping people—the one thing that would make life for me worth living. I even began to keep a journal that I wrote in every night. I was developing more self-esteem. I sensed it and other people noticed it. I missed my grandmother, but really I wanted Denise back. She was on drugs; I grew angry wondering if that man she was seeing put her on them. But soon I learned to let it go. I put it away.

Scott and I did go to an AA meeting later on that week together and I heard a lead that would later change my thinking even further and my life. The young man was an ex-con. He first started out saying that he tried to overdose several times as a means of suicide because he was addicted to so many drugs he couldn't stop using at first. So he overdosed on purpose. As he told his story, my mind began to wander. I thought about my father and my mother and things my grandmother used to tell me. It was as if I could hear her voice again. By the end of his talk, my mind had focused back to his concluding remarks as he talked about how he was able to forgive others and how to stop placing blame. Somehow later that night I began to understand that maybe my father committed suicide as means of a way out, to rid himself of his addiction problem. All this time I had hated him for things he had done. He was an addict, he was sick, he could not help himself and maybe he beat my mama because he felt guilty about the way he was leading his own life. Maybe he beat my mama because he couldn't confront his own problems. I felt I had to forgive him, but it was going to be hard, but I felt if I had the desire, then that was half the battle, a battle that was to be won in a different place. The next couple of days were to be a little easier for me, with the help of some friends in AA. I came out of it. I made friends with a man name William Ferguson, a man from Cleveland. He'd come down every week and help run the AA meetings I would go to. He was a lot older than me, maybe in his early fifties. He'd tell me things like, "You wanna stay sober when you leave here, don'tcha?"

I'd say "yeah" waiting for him to wave that magic wand over my head and then he'd say, "Don't pick up that first drink," and he also told me to stay around sober people. He gave me his number and I kept in contact with him. He was funny, a lot of times he made my day. He would often talk about alcohol and its effect on the mind and body. How we do strange and unusual things while under the influence. I respected him and later on he became my sponsor. I finally received my GED. Mama and Jimmy came to see me. Mama kept bragging about how beautiful my daughter was. She never missed an opportunity to tell me how bright and smart she was. She would show me pictures of her since no young children were allowed to visit.

When it was Scott's time to leave, we exchanged phone numbers.

"Now, when you need to talk, just call," he said. "My girlfriend lives in Jersey." We shook hands. I was going to miss him. I had other friends, but they weren't quite like Scott.

"You be cool," I told him.

I never quite understood Scott; he had a good head on his shoulders, he was white which means he had a opportunity that me as a black man doesn't have in this world, yet he was a dope addict, and the biggest problem is, that I felt he was going back to it. I shook my head and reminded myself to stop being so judgmental. I realized from watching others people, it's a hard lifestyle to give up. I'll never forget him.

Later on that week, a guard came and called my name I got up and he led me down the corridor to a room. As I entered there was a slightly balding man dressed in a gray jacket and a pair of khakis with a tie.

"Jeremiah Washington, I'm Ben, Ben Neilson, an attorney for Neilson and Associates."

We shook hands as I heard the door slam tight. I looked over to see if the guard had left; he was standing on the other side of the door.

"Please sit down." I sat. "I'm here because we had a very interesting development happen over the course of three hours. There was an Officer Gaynor, Mary Anne Gaynor was his sister who was of course Rufus's mother. Officer Gaynor was arrested today with some other officers in a sting operation. The whole thing started when an anonymous tip was given to the police, which led to a six month investigation. Officer Gaynor and few others were involved in a drug trafficking ring. We also believe several of those officers were involved in tampering with evidence that had to do with your case. An arresting officer named Johnson, he's ready to testify that during your arrest there was use of obsessive force in order to make you to confess to the murder as a part of his plea bargain."

"So you're saying he didn't die from trauma from the fight?"

"Exactly. Rufus died of a drug overdose. We have the confession from the coroner that falsified his records for Officer Gaynor so people wouldn't discover the fact that Rufus was selling drugs for him. Officer Johnson, the arresting officer, said they found Rufus with drugs, and a large amount of money that they kept. Rufus was an active cocaine addict. He was probably pumping himself up with the drugs he sold for his uncle." He reached in his briefcase and took out a paper. "Officer Atkinson asked me to talk to you, and he and some other officers would assist us in your case and getting your release." I began to smile.

"We have to go to court first. Is this your mother's address and phone number?" I looked at the paper and said yes. "Good, just so you will know, it's going to be on the news tonight. I don't think it will hurt our case any…. Here's my card and my toll free number." He handed me a small beige card with blue printing on it. "Of course we'll be looking to sue the state for wrongful imprisonment." I held the card in one hand looking at it in wonder. I looked back at him.

"Yes, we'll want to sue," I repeated. "Oh yeah, for how much?" I asked.

"We'll work out the details after the trial; we want to make sure you get out of here okay."

"Yeah." I sat with the card in hand.

"Okay, Mr. Jackson. We'll see you in a few days." He held out his hand for me to shake it. I extended my right arm and shook his hand. I could hardly believe it; this wasn't supposed to happen.

It was ten o'clock when the news came on and it was just as Mr. Neilson said; it was all over the news and on every channel. Even the World News carried the story and then they began talking about me. The code of silence had been broken; the newscaster went on delivering the story. Pat sat in amazement. "That you, Jeremiah?"

"Yeah," I said, "that's me." I hadn't felt like this in a long time; it was as if something good would happen. I could barely get to sleep when the lights went out. I sat pondering what the lawyer said all night.

It was about 2:00 a.m. I got a rude awakening; two guards came to my cell; lights were shining in my face.

"What's this about?" I asked.

"There seems to be a problem with you threatening an officer here."

"What officer? I never said nothing."

"Go with them," Pat said.

"Look, I never said anything. This is a mistake," I said as I got down from my bunk.

I got up and the officers took me by the arms and escorted me to the isolation cell and locked me inside.

I couldn't understand how could this be. *I'll never get out of here; they could say I died for all I would know.* I believe three weeks went by and I heard someone at my cell. It was Shortie. I heard the door unlock. "Look at this," he said smiling.

"Man, they put me in here for no reason," I said as I raised off the floor.

"Protective custody, man," Shortie said. "Officer Atkinson said he wanted you out alive."

The day of the trial, I could have fell asleep in my cornflakes. I managed to get through till it was time to see my lawyer. I spent an hour getting ready for the trial. I was feeling confident that this was it. I went into court with the reassurance from my lawyer I wouldn't be back to the prison. I had on my orange jumpsuit they made us wear in the prison. This was a lot different because I had a jury, not a magistrate, and there were people that were allowed in the courtroom besides my mother. I turned to look around the courtroom. Jimmy was there with three other officers all in uniform. They all smiled with their thumbs up. They argued my case for about two hours. The officers took the stand and there were witnesses that I never heard of. The doctor and coroner's office confessed of falsifying records and said that Rufus died of a drug overdose.

Then one of the girls that was in the hallway at the time the fight started she stated he did have a knife. Claiming then no one took her seriously. They were taking her seriously now; she was a social worker at a hospital. At the end of the trial, I entered a plea of not guilty to the charges of manslaughter. The jury deliberated for fifteen minutes and came back. As the judge read the verdict, I held my breath. They found me not guilty. I didn't think I heard them right. I looked at my mother; she and Jimmy's wife were laughing, holding each other's hands jumping up and down. I was free. I was so happy I hugged my lawyer.

Journalists flooded the Justice Center, surrounding me, begging for a comment. My mother and Jimmy and his wife reached over and hugged me. Then Jimmy, my mother and I thanked the lawyer and the other officers that helped with my case. We got into the car and left. Finally, that segment of my life was behind me now and I was on my way home. I couldn't help thinking, *Boy, I wish my grandmother would have lived to see this day.*

Chapter 11

Freedom for me was scary. I didn't know quite what to expect, but it felt good. I was twenty-one now and looking forward to meeting my daughter for the first time. And Mama was planning a get together at our house. God had placed some powerful examples in my life... for that I was grateful.

Mama was happy, but the house wasn't the same without April. She couldn't make the trial; she had finals, but she was to graduate from college this year. Thinking of my grandmother and closest friends dead, I sat on my favorite spot on the couch. Mama came downstairs holding my daughter Jasmine's hand. Jasmine was five years old, her hair carefully braided, and barrettes were placed in it. I had never seen her in person before.

"Do you know who this is?" my mother asked her smiling. Jasmine shook her head no.

"This is your daddy, give your daddy a hug." It was a real good feeling to have my five-year-old hug me. I was so happy I cried within myself.

"Show your daddy your picture, Jasmine." She held the picture up to my lap and explained to me the big man with the hat was me and other person next to me was "Mommy" and the little person next to her mommy was her. They were primitive forms of stick people; I thanked her and hugged her again.

"Jeremiah, you can rest if you want. You must be tired. You have really gotten big!"

I smiled and answered, "That's from pumpin' all that iron," holding my arm, flexing my muscle.

Jasmine was busy coloring on the floor. I was really amazed; she was a miracle, her hands moving gracefully across the paper. She could speak so well. I was proud she was my daughter.

I was so tired from the day's activities I decided I did need a nap, so I ended up going upstairs after all. Thought about calling J.C. when I remembered he was dead.

I called William.

"I'm at home," I said when he answered.

"Great," he said. "You have any plans for the evening; you want to catch a meeting or something?"

"Yeah, a meeting sounds good," I said.

"Pick you up at seven-thirty tonight." I gave him my address and we hung up. I was glad to have something to do. I looked out my window and there was Jasmine playing with some other children, digging in dirt with these sticks. It was early in the spring and she was just about to stick a handful of mud in her mouth. I yelled out my window.

"Hey!" I surprised her. "Don't you put that mud in your mouth." She looked up and saw me; she dropped the lump of mud from her hands and said "okay" and I watched as she and her friends looked for something else to do.

I went downstairs; Mama was on the phone while she was fixing dinner. I announced to them I was going to a meeting that evening at seven-thirty. I missed having my sister around; it just wasn't the same here without her, but she would be graduating soon. I remember Mama mentioning that she had a job set up in Boston teaching somewhere once she graduated. I was staring off into space when my mother asked me to take the macaroni and cheese out of the oven. I grabbed the oven mitts and took out the dish of hot macaroni and cheese. After which I went and checked on Jasmine. I knew people would be due here around four o'clock.

There was Jasmine riding on a big wheel. when she saw me she said, "Daddy, I want to come inside."

"Okay." Then I heard her ask Tanya if she wanted to come over her. Tanya said yes.

"Daddy, can Tanya come in?"

"Ask your grandmother," I said. So she ran inside. Tanya stood there fidgeting with her feet, snatching leaves off the bushes.

"You Jasmine's daddy?" she asked.

"Yes," I answered.

"Where you been?"

"Out of town." She just sat there smiling at me as if she knew I was lying. Jasmine came to the door and told her little friend that it was okay for her to come in, and in they went, giggling and talking.

I couldn't get used to it. I stayed outside to reflect upon the good times I had on that street. After I came back from daydreaming, I tried to sleep, but couldn't, so I went inside and watched some TV. It was about three o'clock and someone knocked on the door. it was a woman.

"Hi, I'm Tanya's mother, I live next door." Mama came out of the kitchen and into the living room.

"Oh, come on in, Gloria. This is my son Jeremiah."

"Hi," she said.

I really wanted to say, *Baby, are you single?* but I just smiled and said, "Hello, nice to meet you." At least I exercised a little self control.

"Come on, Tanya, it's time to come home." Tanya dropped her crayon and was about to leave when Gloria reminded her to help clean up their mess. After she and Jasmine put away their toys and crayons, she took her mother by the hand and they headed for the door.

"It was nice meeting you," she spoke smiling.

I smiled back and let them out of the house and watched them go home.

"When did she move in?"

"About a year ago."

"How old is she?"

"I don't know, Jeremiah."

"Maybe I could take her out sometime?"

"Maybe you should concentrate on takin' care of your child," Mama said sarcastically.

It was going on four o'clock when people started to come over. Pastor Brown, Jimmy and his wife, Rob and J.C.'s mother. Mama was there at the door to greet them.

When it was time for dinner, Pastor Brown said the blessing. "Lord, we thank you at this time that our son Jeremiah is with us today. We thank you, Lord, for bringing him home safely. We pray that you will guide his footsteps and strengthen him, oh Lord. Amen." I looked around and everyone began to eat. Jimmy began to talk.

"Jerry, I'd really like you to come back and work for me. Can you start, say, tomorrow?"

"Okay."

"You could be my right-hand man. Sometimes I go to the centers and recruit young men who want to work. I'd give you a raise and you could still have the weekends off."

I nodded. I was really glad that Jimmy thought of me that way. I would have a job.

"Sister Washington, everything is so good. Oh, what a friend we have in Jesus. When I was your age, Jeremiah, I had no direction. One night I bent on my knees and said, 'Jesus, make a way for me,' and he did. For Jesus said, 'I came not to call the righteous, but the sinner to repentance.'"

"Yes, sir," my mother added.

So I sat listening to Pastor Brown, but I wasn't ready to go to church, but what he said sounded promising. Anyway, I looked over there where Jasmine was sitting; she had been dropping spoonfuls of mash potatoes in her lap, so I went over and began to wipe her off. She told me she was finished. I let her down from her high chair and went back to finish my meal. After everyone ate, we sat around and talked. Mama talked about April and how we would go down and see the graduation ceremony. While the women talked, Pastor Brown, Jimmy and I went into the living room. I told them I was going to a meeting later on that evening.

"I knew a deacon who went to those meetings. You wouldn't have realized he was the same person. It's a wonder what God can do."

Jimmy told us he and his wife needed to leave. Pastor Brown offered his services.

"You come down to the church and we'll talk."

"Okay." I told Jimmy I would see him tomorrow at six a.m. Mrs. Elliott and Mrs. Campbell complimented me on how I looked as they went out the door. But they stayed there talking to Mama for fifteen minutes, when they left and Mama closed the door. It had been a long day. I went upstairs to get ready for this meeting. Mama brought me some new clothes that could fit— I had gained so much weight in prison—so I put on a sweater and a pair of slacks and shoes. I went straight to the mirror in the bathroom to brush my hair. I gazed upon myself; I still considered myself to be handsome I was muscular. I had a goatee and mustache, close haircut. I made my way downstairs and Mama looked at me.

"Son, you look very nice."

"Thanks," I answered.

"Here, turn around," she said. I turned around. "Your tag is hanging out." I could feel her tucking the tag in on the back of my neck. Then again she said, "You look very nice." I could see the look of approval shining in her eyes.

"I'll be back about nine o'clock." I sat on the couch waiting for William. I closed my eyes and dozed off. When I awoke, I heard the door open. I could hear my mother talking.

"Hi, I'm Georgia, Jeremiah's mother, and you must be William. Come on in. I heard a lot about you." He tapped me on the knee.

"You ready?"

Still drowsy I said, "Yeah, I'm ready." I yawned and proceeded to stand up. I looked at William; he was a towering six foot four, he had to bend down just so his head wouldn't hit our ceiling. I left with William, my cologne reeking.

"Man, what did you do, take a bath in that stuff?"

I laughed. "I guess I did overdo it." I looked over and he was rolling down his window for air, chuckling to himself.

"Any women going to be at the meeting we're going to?" I asked.

"Why?" William answered.

"I'd like to meet someone."

"Look, Jeremiah, concentrate on your sobriety right now; hold off on those relationships," William explained.

"How long should I hold off?" I asked.

"A year."

"I don't think I can wait a year, William."

"You can; you'll be busy doing other things. Focus on your sobriety and everything will fall into place," he said. I wasn't thoroughly convinced, but I followed William's advise like a blind man follows his seeing-eye dog… trusting his input.

Chapter 12

It was June, and April's graduation was coming up. Mama and I got ready for the trip. I rented a car from the car rental that day. I remember the drive home it was warm. I could tell it was going to be a good day. The ceremony was at 7:00 and it was already 4:00. I tried to get Mama to hurry, so we could meet April before they marched.

"Come on, Mama, you look fine." I could tell she was nervous. Jasmine was dressed in a pink dress, white patent leather shoes, and a white patent leather purse to match.

"Okay."

"Come on."

"I have to lock the house." She stood outside the door, dressed in a white skirt with a lime green blouse with ruffles in the front, white sandals, and a lime green and white hat. She wore hats everywhere. After she locked the door, she checked it, I honked.

"I'm coming, my goodness." She had her purse to the side as she climbed in the car.

"Okay, you've got everything 'cause we're not coming back." She checked her purse.

"I just wanted to make sure I had my camera," she said.

"You got it?"

"Yes I have it."

"Good," and I took off. Kent was only a hour away, but when we got there we ran into a crowd at the parking lot. It took us half an hour to get into a parking space it was so crowded. Finally we parked and we got out the car.

Mama grabbed Jasmine's hand with her right hand, and placed her left hand on her hat and led us across the parking lot to the entrance of the school.

I was looking for April when Mama said, "There she is." I saw her talking to one of her schoolmates.

"April!" Mama shouted.

"April!" Jasmine echoed. I noticed that April turned around and came towards us.

"Mama," she hugged her.

"Jerry," she smiled. "It's so nice to see you." She kissed me on the cheek.

"Hi, Auntie."

"Hi, Jasmine, how are you?" She picked her up and swung her around. "How's my big girl?"

"I'm fine. I got a new purse, Auntie, and shoes." Jasmine showed her.

"And they are so pretty. I bet your daddy got those for you." Jasmine stood nodding her head yes. Then April turned towards me and Mama. "It's only five o'clock, but they have refreshments in the lobby."

"Oh, let me take a picture of you," Mama said.

Mama took pictures of us while we stood outside about. An hour passed when April said they had to get ready for the ceremony, so Mama and I looked for a seat in the auditorium. We found one not high up off the ground, because Mama was scared of heights.

The ceremony lasted for about three hours. We listened to a talk about making great achievements by the guest of honor, a minister I had never heard of. It was a nice speech and it even motivated me. After he spoke, the ceremony was over. We went to meet April outside. Mama was so happy she ran up to April and hugged her and then took more pictures. "You are coming home with us?" I asked her.

"Well, I was going to Boston with one of my friends. She lives there. Well you know I got a job there teaching at one of the elementary schools. I'm going to look for a house."

"Oh." I turned to Mama.

"Okay, honey. We'll see you when you get back." Mama hugged April goodbye and we left. When we got home, I guess it was midnight. As I lay in the bed, I swore I could hear Mama in her bedroom talking to my grandmother telling her about the graduation.

The next day I got up for work. When we were finishing up our job, I pulled Jimmy aside before we left on the truck.

"You want to get something to eat?"

ANGELS ONLY STAND
WHERE CHERUBIM TAKE FLIGHT

"Yeah, sure we can go over to McDonald's."

When we got there, I sat down with my food and he sat on the opposite side. "I thought maybe I should be going to church, you know, but every time I think about it I back down. I just don't think I can make the commitment. You know, being good all the time."

"My father would always tell me real religion is in your heart, a church is just a building. Look at Jesus; the people who had him crucified, they were priests, the people who were supposed to uphold the church. The people who Jesus felt empathy for were the sinners, outcasts. You know, Jeremiah, sometimes we spend our lives seeking something that is right there in front of us." Then he took a bite of his sandwich and the changed the subject. "Hey, Saturday I want you to come to a baseball game. Some of the officers in the department are having a game against another precinct. You'll be our guest of honor."

"That sounds good."

Me and Jimmy left the restaurant, and he dropped me off at home. I was feeling good that day.

Saturday arrived and Jimmy picked up Mama and me; we left Jasmine next door. We arrived at the baseball field about ten o'clock. It was a clear day and not a cloud in sight. We all gathered in the lodge near the field. The women and some of their husbands were barbequing hot dogs and hamburgers, they had a spread of potato salad, chips, baked beans, and watermelon. I was looking at how good everything looked, when Jimmy came up behind me and said, "We'll eat later. Come on, the game is about to start."

As guest of honor, I threw out the first pitch.

I sat on the stands and cheered for Jimmy's team to win. It was the ninth inning and they were tied. I watched as the opposing team went up to bat. We hoped that they would not score, but one of the opposing team's best batters was up. When he hit that ball, I knew that Jimmy's team would lose. He hit a home run, they made three more points and the game was over.

Nobody stayed sad for long because of the food; we were ready to eat. I grabbed a plate and began filling it with food, along with a can of strawberry cherry pop, and went out of the lodge, sitting at a picnic table in the shade of a tree. Jimmy came to join me after he got his plate. When he sat down I began to speak.

"I owe you a lot, Jimmy, what makes you...." It wasn't coming out right; I started again. "What made you look after me and Mama all while I was locked up? I mean, you were there for me when I needed someone the most. Why?"

"It's funny you asked me that," he said, and then he looked at the ground and then back at me, except he now he had a serious look on his face. "Before all this, I was a doctor. I worked at a clinic. We lived in New Jersey, nice house." He stared at he ground. "I hated it, my life. My wife, someone I didn't even know anymore, and I hated the world I was in. Then my son came up missing, he'd be about your age now, and no one could find him. After he was missing a week, I prayed and I asked the Lord if he helped me find my son whether he was dead or alive, I promised him I would be my brother's keeper. Well, the next day they found him dead at the beach in a wooded area. I quit my job at the hospital and became a cop. My wife thought I was crazy; she even threatened to leave." He looked at me and laughed, "She didn't though; we're still together."

I stared at him. I couldn't believe the story; it sounded so familiar. I sat speechless. He patted me on the back and said, "You'll understand one day."

"I think I do already."

I thanked him and told him he was like a father to me and that I loved him and would never forget his kindness. I wouldn't have made it without him. He looked at me and said, "I know."

"How long did he know?" I asked.

"Your grandmother told me at church," he explained, "and I first thought that's a little strange, them giving you a statement to sign right in the middle of nowhere. At first I didn't want to believe it, but Gaynor had a reputation, plus there're rumors about Rufus and dealing in drugs. So I watched him, I camped out at his front steps in the morning, and watched him go to the bathroom at night. And one day I struck pay dirt and that's when I believe he knew I was watching him, because when I went into the grocery store and I ran into him, that's when I think he had some inmates try to kill you. Anyway, after I had enough evidence, I sent in an anonymous tip about his suspicious activity. It blew their operation wide open. They falsified the coroner's report because they didn't want them to look for Rufus's supplier.

"Jeremiah, have you ever seen someone that has overdosed."

"No."

"Well, it can cause cardiac arrest. Look, I know you get conditioned that all cops are good and when they do something illegal it's hard for people to understand that, but what they are doing is hiding behind the integrity of the badge. The policeman's badge is supposed to be a badge of honor, courage and righteousness. I've seen sometimes when a crime is committed, there's so much pressure to catch the criminal, even if it means blaming someone that is innocent."

"So you're saying there are more people like me."

"That's exactly what I'm saying. Sometimes you can lose sight of what's important, especially when you are trying to make a name for yourself."

"Well I just wanted to say…."

One of the officers at the game walked up on us. "Come on, fellas, we're about to get started." We got up and headed for the picnic area.

"I'll tell you later."

"Okay." Jimmy began walking towards the lodge and I followed closely behind him, wondering what they were going to do next. We sat down on the table towards the front.

Officer Blithe stood in front behind a podium. "If everyone could quiet down, we are going to start." The crowd silenced.

"First, I'd like to speak on behalf of the department and policemen everywhere, and thank the guest of honor, Jeremiah Washington, and present him with scholarship money to start him off in his career to get a degree in social work." Everyone was cheering and I looked at Jimmy. He was signaling for me to go up to the front.

"Jeremiah, Jimmy said you wanted to become a social worker to help troubled teens and keep them out of prisons and detention homes. Well, we'd like to present you with a check for $6,000 to start you off in your efforts to regain your life back." Everyone cheered; I stood and walked over to the podium and said, "I'd like to thank everyone for helping me."

I was so overcome by emotion I just held up the check and said, "Thanks," and I looked at my mother and saw she was crying. I almost broke down myself. I sat back down next to her and Jimmy.

"Still speaking on behalf of the department, we would like to give this plaque to Officer Atkinson for the Officer of the Year Award. Officer Atkinson, you are what we strive for. This plaque indicates there are still good policemen out there trying to do the right thing. Let's be conscious of or actions when we serve the public as we become the majority and officers like Gaynor become the minority." Everyone cheered; he lowered his arms to quiet the crowd.

"This is Officer Atkinson's last week here on the force." I think the words "last week on the force" caught everyone including myself by surprise. I knew this was his life's work; he loved this job. I was puzzled as to what all this meant. Officer Blithe continued to talk over the crowd's disappointed oohs and aahs.

"We hope you will accept this plaque on behalf of the Cleveland Police Department."

Jimmy stood up and walked over to Officer Blithe and accepted the plaque and began to give a speech.

"I'd like to thank everyone for this honor. As officer Blithe said, I am leaving the force. I am sorry to say after the flood of death threats, I thought it best to leave on the request of my wife. Being a cop was easy; being a good cop took effort; being one of the few African-American cops was tough. Sometimes just trying to be accepted has its drawbacks. We want to be loyal even when our integrity is at stake. Sometimes we make someone out to be a criminal when the only crime is our own actions and our own thoughts. I guess what I'm trying to say is, Jeremiah, I'm glad you're home. You are like the son I never had and I love you." He held up his plaque. "Thank you."

The crowd stood and clapped. Jimmy shook Officer Blithe's hand and came and sat back next to his wife. When the people had returned to their regular activities, walking up to Jimmy asking him and his wife questions, hugging as I overheard them telling them how much he'd be missed, he and his family, Officer Blithe walked up to me and patted me on the shoulder. "If you ever decide to become a cop, let me know."

Since I was always taught to never turn down an opportunity, I shook his hand and said, "Thank you. It's hard work and you never know when the day comes when you don't come back home. It's just one of the hazards, of the job, I mean." Then he shifted his weight on the sides of his shoes.

"Social work is an honorable job, also."

I answered "yes," but my mind was far away at this point. I was thinking of Jimmy. "Jimmy's had an impact on my life."

"He's a fine officer; his conscience led him to do the right thing." He shook my hand and said, "The best of luck in the future, Jeremiah." Then he walked away. Mama stood by smiling.

She and Carol were talking. She kept saying, "This is so wonderful, Carol." I watched as the guests were all getting ready to leave. It was already about five in the evening; people were saying their goodbyes. Jimmy approached us.

"You all ready to go?"

"Yes, honey, we're ready." I watched as Jimmy hugged his wife as we walked towards the car. Mama and Carol had their own conversation going.

"You didn't tell me you were leaving."

"I didn't tell anyone. I made the decision fifteen minutes before I stood up."

I looked at him and said, "Really?"

"Yeah, I really wanted to surprise my wife. Now I can devote my time to the landscaping business full time."

We all got in the car and I wondered at the kindness all the way home. I was so lucky to get money to go to college.

When we arrived home, Mama went next door to get Jasmine and I went to my room to write in my journal about the day's events and my thoughts concerning them, however few they were. I couldn't risk putting everything on paper, fearing someone might find them, and know what's really on my mind. I could picture my mother coming down the steps or better yet standing on the front porch as I would come home from work. *Jeremiah, what nonsense is this?* I placed it in my closet for safe keeping as I heard Jasmine coming through the door, thinking no one would find it there, except maybe my mother, who could find a needle in a haystack, if you put it there to hide it. I was on my way downstairs and Mama met me at the bottom of the stairs.

"You upstairs already?"

"Yeah, I had to do something."

"Like what?"

Then I realized I told on myself. "Nothing."

"You went upstairs to do something but it was nothing that you did. That is the most ridiculous thing I had ever heard. You're starting to sound as silly as your sister."

"I had to straighten up my room," I said lying.

"Oh, the truth comes out. Jasmine needs some new shoes and a coat for the winter."

"Okay," I answered, trying to calculate how much everything was going to cost in my head.

"She also needs to get into nursery school this fall; she's old enough.

"If you wait till Labor Day, you might be able to find some things on sale. She'll need some church dresses and other things. You can give me the money, I'll shop for her, or we can all go together one evening."

"I'll give you the money," I said because it was never for just an evening with Mama; it was more like the whole day, or two days, one day to shop, the next day taking things back.

"All right, sweetie, let's go in the kitchen to let Grandma wash your hair."

I watched as Jasmine was guided in the kitchen by my mother. I couldn't understand it; they were like two peas in a pod.

The rest of the summer along with my working and taking care of Jasmine, William took me to lots of meetings. I even went to some on my own, and a year passed in no time. That's when I realized William was right. I did have plenty to do and now I could date, but who? I had met lots of girls there at those meetings, but there was one, Virginia, I really could see myself with her. I like the way she wore her hair and she wasn't too bad-looking with nice legs to match. So I talked to William about it. I told him I thought she'd make a good wife.

He laughed and said, "You don't even have a car to present to your new wife." I realized he was right. I asked Jimmy the next day if I could borrow his car that weekend so I could take her out; Jimmy said yes. I was in seventh heaven. I really liked this girl, so I called her up and asked her out and she said yes. I would pick her up at 6:30. I planned a nice evening with dinner included. I couldn't believe I was going on a date; it had been so long. She was two years sober I had only fifteen months.

Going to school was going to be tough and I'd often think about what Mama would always tell me: *You don't have to go to college to make good money, you could take up a trade and still do well.* That 6,000 dollars would help a great deal, so I looked up some nearby colleges to go to part time or something, just to get myself started.

Well anyway, Saturday arrived and I went to pick up Virginia in a '78 station wagon. Of course, I had to admit to her it wasn't my car. I worried that maybe it wasn't impressive enough. I hoped she wouldn't give me the brush off because of the car. But surprisingly everything went really well. She talked about her son and her job; she worked as a receptionist at a doctor's office. She was a year older than me. We talked so much that we were late for the movie, but in spite of that everything went fine. And she at the end of the date smiled and before she left the car made it a point to tell me how much she enjoyed herself, and how she would like to do it again. I kissed her on the cheek and she got out of the car still smiling, then she ran into the house. I watched her as she went in. I was mesmerized.

I was soon able to buy my own car and since I knew how to work on cars, I purchased a used Buick and stopped using Jimmy's car.

Chapter 13

It was December when my sister called Mama and invited us to Christmas dinner and vacation in Boston. When Christmas vacation came for Jasmine, we decided to leave for Boston. Mama asked our next door neighbor's daughter Tanya if she could come along to help keep Jasmine company.

I decided to take the turnpike. I had never driven so far before. Taking William's advise, I bought a CB radio before I made the trip. If I had road trouble, I could call the police or an ambulance. While the kids were in the back seat, my mother and I listened to the radio trying to decipher the language that the truckers were using, being cautious of the speed traps along the way. We stopped a Burger King for the second time. It was Jasmine's favorite fast food restaurant. She wouldn't eat anything else. I came out of the restaurant with the food and two crowns. I handed the crowns to the girls, and helped them place them on their heads.

"Daddy, I'm a queen," Jasmine smiled.

"Yes, Jasmine, you're a queen."

As we ate, Jasmine sat in the back seat, shouting orders to Tanya and her imaginary subjects. Dictating to both how fast and how many French fries could be eaten at a time.

Mama glanced at me. "Listen to her," she chuckled, mocking her, saying, "Sure hate to live in her kingdom."

I started the car continuing with the trip; we were sixty miles from Boston. We started out at ten-thirty this morning so we expected to arrive at about seven-thirty if we didn't get lost. April got off work at five and arrived home about six o'clock and we were making good time. We drove up into the driveway and there was April to greet us. As I got out of the car, Mama and April were already giving each other hug and kisses. April looked at my daughter. "Jeremiah, she looks just like Denise."

"Yeah."

April opened the front door to her house. When I went inside, I looked around. "This is a nice place, girl. What kinda of money are you makin'?"

"Not enough."

"More than me, that's for sure," I said as I watched Mama look around.

"Is this the dining room set you told me about?"

"Yes, Mama, I got it for seventy-five percent off. The furniture store was having a clearance."

"You got a good deal. It looks like it's worth over two thousand."

"Yeah, well, we won't go into that. Hi, ladies, would you like some ice cream?" Jasmine and Tanya nodded yes. They acted like the Bobbsie twins. Jasmine came over by me.

"Who is this, April?" I picked up a picture of her and a man embracing one another.

"That's Gerald."

"Which is why she doesn't have time to visit," Mama added.

"Your boyfriend?"

"No, just a friend. You all can sleep upstairs. Come on, Jerry, you can take the luggage upstairs to the room."

"Can't I rest? I'll take it up in a minute."

"Sure," April answered. I watched Jasmine and Tanya eat their ice cream in a bowl April had given them. "You didn't ask me if I wanted some."

"She didn't ask anyone if they wanted any," Mama said.

"I asked the kids; you all can get your own." I made my way into her kitchen, found a bowl and went over to the refrigerator. I could overhear Mama talking to April. I think she was mad because April never came to visit or even called much.

I took a few scoops of ice cream and then came back into the living room. I handed Mama the bowl. "I'll go get that luggage." I went to get the luggage out of the trunk, and carried it up the stairs. April told me that Mama and Jasmine and Tanya could sleep in her room and I could sleep in the guest room. I placed the luggage in the rooms and went downstairs.

"You all want to go get something to eat? There's a place here that serves really good seafood."

"Sure. Mama, you want to go?" I said as I watched her expression change.

"Okay," she said.

April suggested that we take her car so we packed into April's Honda and were on our way. I couldn't help notice the houses were different from the ones in Cleveland and the streets were made of brick.

I held the children's hands as we got out of the car and crossed the parking lot as we headed for the entrance to the restaurant. Once inside, I looked around; it was nice but I felt a bit underdressed. After we stood in line for twenty minutes, the hostess showed us a table; we got booster seats for the girls.

"This is nice; this place is real nice," Mama commented.

"Hi, April." I looked up and there was a gentleman in a suit.

"Hi, I didn't expect to see you here." I looked at Mama. I thought to myself, *Oh brother.*

"Mama, this is Gerald." April was glowing.

"Hi, Gerald, how are you?" Mama said.

"Who are you here with?" Gerald said.

"Just some friends," April said.

Before she could say it, I asked, "Would you like to sit with us?"

"Oh no," Gerald said.

"Oh come on," I said. "We got plenty of room, don't we, April?"

"You can sit with your friends if you want," she replied.

"Well, if you don't mind, I'll sit here," Gerald said.

I smiled to myself because I had never seen April act so sneaky. I spent the rest of the evening listening to how Gerald was a marketing executive and how he helped her with her investments. I looked at Mama; that's when I believe it struck a nerve, when I saw Mama push her empty plate away. "April, I'm ready to go."

"Mama, everyone hasn't finished eating, though."

"April, we've been finished for an hour now, we're just sitting here just listening to you talk, now I'm ready to go."

We got the kids together and Mama and I walked to the car. "The nerve of that man! I believe if that man asked her to kiss his toes, she'd be takin' off his shoes. Don't tell her I said that."

"I won't, Mama. He looks like a good man."

"All he wants is her to make these investments, he ain't doin' nothin' but takin' advantage of her, makin' money off her. Look at her."

I saw her and Gerald kissing right outside the front entrance. *So this is what it was all about.* We were in for a tense evening, I could tell.

"Daddy, I'm cold. I'm ready to go home."

Mama left the car and went to get April, shouting at her, "Look, we are ready to go, it's...."

I just stood shaking my head. After I saw Gerald leave, I could hear Mama and April arguing in the cold. April came to the car crying. Mama following close behind got in after her. Everything's quiet and I could hear April sniffling. After we leave the parking lot for a while, Mama blurts out, "I don't know what you crying about, why don't you just hand him your paycheck and be done with it? I'm trying to tell you right." April was silent. I was silent; the kids had fallen asleep. It wasn't until we had gotten home and everyone settled in that I went in the kitchen and talked to my sister.

"That wasn't going to work."

"You caught on, huh?" April said.

"Yeah, like a piece of wood that snags onto a sweater," I said.

"Well, I'm trying to convince her that he isn't a bad person."

"You know Mama. I thought he was just a friend anyway."

"Jeremiah, I want to get married. Why does he have to please her? She's not going to marry him, I am."

"Well, tell her that then."

"I can't, you know how Mama is. I set this evening up so she could at least see him."

"Well, he seems like a nice man."

"She's angry because I lost some money in an investment that Gerald gave me a tip on."

"You think he's shady?"

"Jeremiah, the stock fell to thirty cents a share. I lost twenty thousand dollars. He lost money, too."

"At least that's what he told you."

"You're starting to sound just like Mama."

"Well, if he's so good to you, why are you trying so hard to please her anyway? Just get married and be done with it."

"Well, maybe I will. No, I can't, his parents want to meet her."

"Look, I don't think his parents want to meet Mama."

"Why?"

"You know how outspoken she is. She'll insult them right to their face and that will be it. And then he won't be marrying you."

"You think they will judge me by my family?"

"Hey, if my daughter was getting married...."

"Well, forget it then. You're right, she would say something sassy and wouldn't care who she offended.

"Like the time I was in school and she came up there because big Linda cut my ponytail in class. And she cussed the principal out because the teacher should have been more aware of what's going on in her class."

"Yeah, see, it was funny then, but now I don't think it'd be too funny, especially if she let his parents know how she feels about their son."

"You're right about that. But the problem is they're coming over tomorrow," and she paused.

"With Gerald?" I answered. "Well, I suppose you can't miss what you never had."

"Jeremiah, that's not funny, just pray for me, please."

"Okay."

It was two in the morning and I excused myself and went to bed. I passed Mama's bedroom and she called me in the room. "Did she say she was getting married?" I was so surprised I told her, "No, Mama."

"Jeremiah, don't lie for your sister, she did say that, didn't she?"

I didn't feel like making this a big issue, especially when I was tired. "Mama—."

"That's all right, Jeremiah. I heard every word." Then I heard her mumble, "That girl is crazy."

"Goodnight, Mama."

"Goodnight."

Were we talking that loud? I had to wonder what would make a person stay up till two in the morning listening to someone else's conversation. Then I quickly remembered how I stayed up listening to my mother and my grandmother. Like they say, the fruit doesn't fall too far from the tree. I was a little like my mother after all. I took my medicine and went to bed.

I was awakened the next morning by Jasmine and Tanya asking me could they go downstairs to eat. I was tired.

"Where's your grandmother?" I asked.

"She not here," they answered.

I got up immediately and put on a robe. I looked in April's room; she wasn't there.

"April," I shouted; no answer. "Come on, let's find something to eat." I looked in the cabinet; nothing but bran cereal.

Great, I have to cook. I went in the refrigerator. *Now I know why she took us out to dinner,* I thought, *she didn't have anything to eat.* I noticed a half of a cantaloupe sitting in the refrigerator like the Lone Ranger, fighting off the enemy, fat and calories.

"You all want some fruit?"

"Yes."

I cut up the cantaloupe. It looked so good even I had a piece. Since my only other choice was the bran cereal, I decided to choose what I thought would be the tastier route.

I was just about to sit down and eat when the telephone rang. "Hello, Hello?" No one answered, just someone breathing heavy on the other end. I had to wonder. No I'm sure my sister was dating a man with more sense than that. Where was April anyway? Where would Mama and she go at eight o'clock in the morning?

After we finished our breakfast, we went into the family room. While the kids watched cartoons, I stood around looking out of the window every once in a while to see if April and my mother had come back.

It wasn't till twelve that I heard the door unlock.

"Come and help us with these groceries." Apparently they had gone shopping. I went out to the car and began to help carry the bags into the house. On the second trip, I grabbed a couple of bags and proceeded to carry them in the house. The bag burst, and all of its contents spilt on the ground. My sister came out to help with the mess.

I noticed there was a magazine with a baby on the front cover. I picked it up; my sister quickly tried to take it from me.

"No." I snatched my hand back so she couldn't grasp it.

"I want to see it." I looked closely at the picture; it was a magazine for new mothers. I looked up at her. "You're pregnant, aren't you?"

April looked up towards the house and I turned around in the same direction to see what she was looking at, and there was Mama standing right there watching us from the front porch.

"Be quiet," she whispered as she snatched the magazine out of my hand.

I began to pick up the cans and frozen food from off the ice-covered driveway and gather them in my hands, carrying them into the house and placing them on the counter.

I could hear them arguing again, this time about the comment I made about her being pregnant. This was not looking good, it was almost Christmas and they were in there fighting like cats and dogs. I went into the living room where they were arguing. "Will you two just stop it."

"Who asked you to come in here and interrupt our conversation?"

"You weren't talking, you were fighting. What if the girls hear you?" Mama looked down and my sister placed her hand on her neck. They both seemed ashamed.

"Mama, April is a grown woman now, you can't run her life like that. Whether she is pregnant or wants to get married." Mama looked surprised. My sister glanced at me, rolled her eyes and shook her head. "Sorry," I said to April, "but you should do what you want; you're grown."

"I am not going to sit idly by as she sits up here and makes a fool out of herself. I don't care if he does make a nice living and if she's pregnant by that sneak,. I tell you what." She threw her hands up and then waved them in the air.

"I'm done with it. You can sit by as everything you worked for goes down the toilet. I don't care, but don't call me when it's time to do your plumbing." She went into the back with the children. I looked at my sister and went out the front door to bring in the remaining groceries.

I felt concerned about my sister, but I knew that she had to live her own life, make her own mistakes; no one could live her life for her. I went to see what my sister was doing after I finished bring the groceries in. I went into the living room and offered to put them away. "You want to talk?"

"Thanks, but no thanks."

"You're mad because I told Mama you want to get married and you're pregnant. How was I supposed to know she didn't know?"

"I'm sorry. It's Christmas eve and the Christmas tree isn't even up."

"Well April, I can put it up and the girls can help decorate it. Is Gerald coming over for Christmas dinner?"

"Well, I thought it might be nice to go over his parents' house for dinner."

"You don't give up too easily, do you?"

"All I want is for her to meet his parents; maybe she'd change her mind about him."

"Are they still coming over today?"

"Well no, but I thought if we—."

"Let me guess, you told them they'd meet her at Christmas?"

"Gerald thought it might be more comfortable for Mama to just to come over there for dinner."

I watched her as she slowly put away the groceries. I picked up a can of green beans.

"Where do these go?"

"Up in the top shelf in the cabinet." After the groceries where put away, we sat in the kitchen.

"So what are you going to do?" I asked.

"About what?" she answered.

"You know, the baby."

"Who says there is a baby?"

"April, look, you can't keep hiding, she's going to know, unless...."

"Unless what?"

"You get an abortion."

"Well, I'm not going to do that."

"So you are pregnant."

"Jeremiah, I didn't want to say anything till Gerald was around. Can't you just wait?"

I looked at my sister; she must really like this fellow. I felt like Mama. In a sense I didn't trust him too much either, but for her sake I'd keep that a secret.

"Well, let's put up the tree," I said rising from my seat.

"Okay, it's in the attic. I'll take you up there and you can bring it down." When we got into her attic, dust was everywhere. I began sneezing.

"You allergic to the dust?"

"A little," I answered I took the box by the end and dragged it down the steps into her living room. "Where do you want it?" I asked.

"Right over there by the fireplace."

I went to get the girls and said, "Who wants to help decorate the tree?"

"I do, I do." The girls abandoned their coloring books and crayons and followed me into the living room. I took out the branches of the artificial tree and told the girls to watch as I put the tree up, and then they could help decorate it. It only took me twenty minutes to put up the tree. My sister brought down the tree ornaments and tinsel. The girls seemed to have a knack for tree decorating; they placed the ornaments on the branches so nicely I thought maybe the art lessons that Jasmine had taken really paid off. April went and made some hot cider and we sat for the rest of the evening drinking hot cider and eating nuts.

"Mama," April said. "Mama, Gerald's parents would like to have you and Jeremiah over for Christmas dinner."

I never saw my sister so determined for my mother's approval.

"Well okay, where does his parents live?"

"They live in Maryland. It's not that far of a drive from here. We'll be there in a couple of hours." Then she turned to me and smiled.

I sent the kids to bed that night and Mama, my sister and I sat up. It was like a family conference. "So what do his parents do?" Mama asked.

"His father is retired; he was a pilot for a commercial airline, and his mother is a nurse; she still works."

"Oh, does Gerald live with them?"

"No, he lives here in Boston. Not far from here.

"He has two older brothers, one who died in a car accident just recently. His funeral was a little over a month ago. His other brother Lawrence is in the military; he's made it a career."

"Oh, what was the name of the brother who died?"

"They called him Bingo, but his real name was Winston."

After that we took the gifts we had brought with us so they would have a little Christmas away from home, and set them out for the girls. Our gifts we opened that night. Mama gave me a sweater, and April gave me a new wallet and some cologne. I bought Mama and April new robes. After we finished putting out the gifts, Mama announced she was going to bed. "You two be sure to tell his parents how excited I am to meet them, okay, April? I'll see you all in the morning."

I was relieved to see my mother acting so calm this evening. I almost believed she wasn't angry, but the reality was I knew she wasn't happy about it; at least she was going to try to be polite. I watched as April set out another bowl of popcorn. "We've eaten so much popcorn I'm a turn into a kernel." She laughed, then her face turned serious.

"How are you?" April asked.

"I'm okay," I answered.

"Mama told me when you first got home, you would stay up in your room until she called you down."

"Yeah I had to adjust to being out of jail. Being in prison for all those years. I'd still be there if it weren't for…."

"Jeremiah, let's just put it that way."

"Yeah, I guess at first I missed my friends I had made in there. I still plan on visiting one day."

April smiled and said, "You making any big plans?"

"Like you? No, not yet, I've thought about it, though. I don't make a nice salary like your Casanova." We laughed. "Her name is Virginia."

"I remember."

"She's a nice girl."

"Mama think so?"

"I guess, we've never had any discussions like you and her, though."

"You must be doing pretty good, then." Then she changed the subject. "It must have been rough in jail."

"Yeah, I got through it though even though I almost died in there."

She hugged me. "I was so afraid when you went in there, I prayed for you every day. When you went it was hard. I remember I was still in high school."

"It's all over with, April. Stop crying."

"It was hard for us after that happened, people avoided us, but our real friends at church supported us, there were others that had been through the same thing. Mama almost lost her job after that."

"She never told me that. I was so young and things were happening so fast then."

"Well, I'm glad your home, that's all."

"So when are you due?"

"In six months," she answered.

"You're three months already?"

She smiled and nodded.

"Does he know?"

"Of course he knows, dummy, that's why he wants to marry me."

"Oh, kind of like a shotgun wedding, except the gun is on you this time."

"I don't feel obligated to marry him. We talked about it and we both agreed marriage was the best solution, that's all."

"Well, you have my permission."

"I didn't know I needed it, but thanks for your blessing, anyhow." She placed her right hand on her chest, looked up at me and said, "I'm honored."

"You're just teasing," I said.

"No, really, Jeremiah. I really appreciate your accepting this whole thing. I only wish Mama would."

"Give her time, things will work out." I realized then I was talking to her the way my grandmother used to talk to me.

"Well, you think we should go to bed? It's almost three in the morning."

"Yeah, sure. I'll see you in the morning."

"Goodnight."

I got up slowly and started to go up the stairs, almost afraid that Mama would still be up. I went past April's room. Everyone was asleep as far as I could tell. I slipped into my pajamas and got in the bed, but not before praying first. I went over the day's events in my head, put in a journal entry, and then lay across the bed with my head on my pillow, wondering how Christmas dinner would turn out. It was probably no wonder we were invited over here this Christmas, so April could reveal this plan slowly to my mother. If she knew Mama half as well as I did, she would know that the term *rationalization* does not exist in my mother's world. Mama was headstrong; she and my grandmother were the most powerful influences in our lives.

Chapter 14

It snowed Christmas day. I was up early with the girls as they opened their gifts. I explained to them Santa would leave something back at home for them also. I don't even think that they heard me, they were so busy giggling and comparing gifts to the other's. A couple of dolls, some board games, a modernized toy oven with utensils, and some clothes my mother and April gave them. I don't think that they even cared about the gifts they'd receive at home; these seemed to satisfy them just as much as if they had gotten a room full of toys; they couldn't be happier. So I got dressed, Mama dressed the girls, everything seemed to go fine until my sister came down with a pair of jeans on and a sweater.

"You're not going like that, are you?" Mama said.

"Yeah, what's wrong with it?"

"I thought you wanted me to meet his family?"

"I do."

"Then why are you dressed like you're going to have lunch with your girlfriends or something?" Mama's hand was on her hips by now.

"Mom, why does everything have to be a big deal with you?"

Mama crossed her arms and said, "I'm not going if you're going to be dressed like that."

"Mom, I really don't have anything else to wear."

"You mean to tell me you make fifty thousand dollars a year and you don't have any dress clothes?"

"Ma—."

"See, this is what I'm talking about; if you're going to introduce your parents to your boyfriend's family, then you should dress better; take a little pride in yourself. If you go like that, I'd just as well stay here."

"Mom, I can't fit into anything else. I've picked up some weight."

"Well, you knew that two weeks ago, why didn't you just buy something special, you've got money."

"Mom, I'm pregnant." I never saw my sister act so sensitive; it must be the pregnancy. She ran upstairs and I went up after her.

She sat on the edge of the bed crying, managing to get out the words, "I cannnn't stannnnnd heeerrrr."

I sat there with my arm around her. "Look, April," I said. "Why don't you just leave her here, okay?"

"I'll be so embarrassed," she said. I had a feeling this would happen, the problem was I didn't know what to do.

"What is she crying about?" I could her my mother yell from downstairs. "Tell her to come on."

"Come on, April, she said let's go." I could hear Jasmine asking her grandmother why Auntie was crying.

We made it downstairs and Jasmine was still asking questions. My mother finally looked down and said, "Look, Jasmine, stay out of grown folks' business." We headed for the Andersons' house for dinner. The car was silent except for the girls in the back seat playing with their Barbie dolls. The dolls were in school and Tanya was able to be the teacher this time, only because she threatened not to play if Jasmine wouldn't let her doll be the teacher. I sat next to them listening to how two young girls were talking like grown women almost. When we reached the Andersons, Gerald greeted us at the door. "Hi, Mrs. Washington, I heard so much about you. I'm Gerald."

I held my breath as my mother gave a flat reply. "I remember." I could tell she wasn't impressed.

As we entered the house, Gerald introduced us to his family. "Jeremiah, Mrs. Washington, these are my parents Adriana and Marshal."

"How are you, Mrs. Washington? Come on in, Jeremiah. You can give me your coats, I'll put them away."

"Hi, Gerald," I said as I shook his hand. "You remember my daughter and her friend?"

"Yes, how are you young ladies?"

"Fine. What is that?" Tanya pointed across the room.

"That's a fish tank. You want to see it?"

"What kind of fish in there?" That was Jasmine's question.

"Well, let's go over there and see." While Gerald showed the children the fish in the tank, Gerald's father came beside me.

"Your daughter?"

"Yes, sir."

"You don't look old enough to have a daughter. Married?"

"No, not yet." I was squirming. I could just imagine my sister being jilted at the altar because of her unwed brother and hotheaded crazy mother.

"Come sit down, all of you, here," Gerald's mother said. "We are so excited to meet your family, April."

"Well thanks for inviting us, Mrs. Anderson," Mama replied.

"Call me Adriana, please."

"Okay, Adriana. You can call me Georgia."

"This is so nice. Is this your daughter, Jeremiah?" Mrs. Anderson asked.

"Yes, that's my daughter Jasmine and our next door neighbor, her best friend Tanya."

"Oh, you girls are so cute. How old are they?"

"Tell Mrs. Anderson how old you are," Mama told them.

"I'm five." Jasmine held up her fingers.

"I'm five, too. My birthday is November 5."

"Oh, so you just had a birthday," Adriana replied.

Tanya smiled and nodded.

"Well, I think dinner is ready. We can all go into the dining room."

"This is a beautiful dining room set, Adriana," Mama commented.

"Yes, we just bought it. I sold April our old one. Were you able to see it?"

"Yes, I saw it." I saw Mama glance at me. I sat down. April continued to smile as if to say, *Please don't spoil this evening.* Gerald sat next to April. The prayer was said and the food was being passed. "So, I understand these two want to get married," Mama began saying.

"Yes, isn't that wonderful? Gerald told us about the plans last month," Mrs. Anderson answered.

"That's nice," Mama answered, then she turned to April and asked her, "When are you planning the wedding?"

"In about four months; that's the only time Gerald can get time off work."

"Why would you wait four months?"

"Mama, because that's what we decided. It's not your wedding."

"Why would you walk down that aisle with your stomach as big as a basketball? You all did know she was pregnant, didn't you?"

Mr. and Mrs. Anderson looked every bit of surprised.

"Mama, I don't believe you sat here tellin' my business in front of my future husband's family."

"You're pregnant and already showing and in four months you're going to get married. How much of your business do you think I'd have to tell?"

"I'm not showing," April protested.

"Well, you can't fit your clothes. I'm sorry, Mr. and Mrs. Anderson, but this whole trip has been full of deceit, lies and ploy just to get me to approve of their sneaky, lowdown plans. Then I get here and find out the only reason they are getting married is because your son has gotten my daughter pregnant."

"Ma, my child deserves to have a father at home."

"I'm not saying that it doesn't, but you should have thought of that before you laid down with him."

"Mrs. Washington, I respect April, and we talked. I told her that if she didn't want to get married, she didn't have to. We love each other. I promise I will take good care of her," Gerald pleaded.

"You gonna talk to me about love and respect? Was it respect when you enticed my daughter to buy some stocks and she lost hundreds of thousands of dollars? But I bet you made your money."

"Mama, it was only forty thousand."

"Did he pay you back? This is making me sick. I'm ready to go."

"Mrs. Washington, you haven't even finished eating. Please."

"Adriana, thanks for the hospitality, but I've had enough. If it isn't her, it's her brother. April, let's go."

"Mama, I'm not going."

"Give me the keys, April, and have Gerald take you home. I'll take Mama home," I said.

"You know the way there?" April asked.

"Just write the directions down, I'll figure it out."

"Can the kids stay here with me? They haven't finished eating."

"If they want, they can stay. You want to stay?" I asked them; they both nodded yes. The vote was unanimous; they were staying.

"Don't give your auntie no trouble, hear?"

Jasmine and Tanya nodded their heads, their mouths full of food.

"I'll see you later." After Gerald got our coats, Mama went outside. I took Gerald aside and said, "You better hope she isn't like her mother." That was my test, let him sweat going down the aisle, with that thought in his mind, because only a fool would marry someone like my mother. My mother wasn't the easiest woman in the world to please. I patted him on the back and said, "Good luck." Gerald gave me a weak smile as he shook my hand. April came up from behind him and handed me a plate of food along with the directions to her house. I thanked Mr. and Mrs. Anderson for the dinner and left. I can't say I was surprised, I had a feeling this would happen, I came mentally prepared. This evening had a very familiar tone to it, yet it had its differences.

    I drove home with the same pace that a man walks on egg shells, very carefully. I didn't want to say the wrong thing to Mama, but I felt April was grown. Why be so hard on her? Couldn't she see April just wanted to please her? I kept my mouth shut the whole ride. When we reached April's house, it began to snow, hard. We had just been caught in the beginning of the storm when I drove into the driveway. I knew they weren't coming home, at least not tonight. The news was broadcasting a snowstorm coming from the west and hitting Boston in full force. By the time I took off my coat and put it in the closet, it was blizzard conditions. I went into April's room and called Virginia. I didn't want to be around Mama right now; to talk to her would be like diffusing a bomb that would go off if the wires weren't taken apart correctly. I prayed Virginia would answer the phone. The phone rang three times, then ten, after that, I knew she probably was in bed because she had to work in the morning. I hung the phone up.

    Well the only option I had was to go in the family room with Mama and finish watching TV. Maybe I'd cheer her up with a bowl of ice cream. April had so much ice cream in her freezer she could open up her own ice cream parlor. She had about ten different flavors: black walnut, chocolate chip, mint chocolate chip, vanilla, chocolate, strawberry, chocolate chip cookie dough, just to name a few, plus she had sherbet orange, lemon and lime, cones, ice cream sandwiches and ice cream bars lined up and down the sides of her freezer. Anyone looking in her freezer could tell she was either crazy or pregnant. I thought she was both since I knew she was pregnant, and she wasn't a very good liar either, but to me someone would have to be crazy to do the things I observed April do since we'd been here.

    The next couple of days at April's were educational. I can't begin to tell you the things I learned here.

Chapter 15

The sun had come out today, but it was still cold. I guess Mother Nature felt guilty for unleashing her fury on us in that snowstorm last night. The only thing that was left was a beautiful cover of snow, a beautiful white winter wonderland. I sat staring out of the window, admiring the snow-covered tree branches while waiting patiently for April to come home. My mother came downstairs and asked were April was.

"She's not here," I said munching on a bowl of Cheerios.

"I'd just as soon take the greyhound bus home." So I sat continuing to eat my Cheerios, quietly giving a lot of thought of what not to say. "You know where the terminal is?" she asked.

"I can find it."

"Good, I'm packing my things. I want to go home."

Mama went upstairs to pack while I looked through the phone book to find out where the bus station was. I called and asked for directions. Writing the directions on a sheet of paper, I thought, *This might be best*. The more April tried to impress Mama, the more Mama retaliated. One thing was for sure, she didn't like Gerald.

Finally she came down. I watched her as she put on her coat.

"I'm ready."

I grabbed the paper, then placed her luggage in the back seat and got into the car.

"Jeremiah, you can tell your sister that if she marries that man, she will not be blessed," she said as I headed out of the driveway. "Yes, sir," she said as she tightened the grip on her purse in her lap. "God surely does not bless her. These kids these days don't listen to their parents and now she's pregnant. Humph."

As I drove, I wondered why she had to bring God into it. Still, on our way to the station, saying only *uh-huh* and *nuh-uh*, she continued to talk, trying not to be too biased, in my opinion. I found it was better not to have an opinion at all, at least not until I could win the argument. When we got to the station, I asked her what time the bus left. She said in about in an hour, but she would wait there. I gave her some money to spend on the trip back, and I left feeling guilty as if it were my fault that she left. She told me she called one of the Sisters from church so someone would be there to pick her up when she got to Cleveland.

"Okay, bye, Mama." I hugged her.

"I'll call when I get home." At first she looked at me as if she were going to cry, then she stiffened her lips and went inside the terminal. I rode back to April's. When I got inside the phone was ringing. I went to answer it, but they had hung up by the time I said *hello*. I fixed myself a bowl of ice cream and ate as I watched a rerun of Bonanza. The phone rang; I picked it up. It was April on her way home. I informed her that Mama had left and we would talk when she got home.

An hour passed when I noticed them pulling into the driveway. I looked and Jasmine and Tanya had on new outfits. It was four o'clock.

"We bought them something else to wear, Gerald's mom's idea."

I looked up and Gerald was right behind her.

"Hey man, what's up?" I said to Gerald, shaking his hand. "I hope they behaved themselves."

"Yeah, they didn't cause any problems. You need anything, babe?"

"No."

"Well, I got work to do," Gerald said turning to April.

"Okay," April answered.

"Okay. I'll call." They kissed each other and Gerald left. April closed the door behind him.

"Look." She held out her hand and danced her fingers around.

"Wait, let me see." I grabbed her hand to take a closer look. She had a ring on her finger. It had to be at least two carats. I leaned back.

"I'm not into that," I said.

"What?"

ANGELS ONLY STAND
WHERE CHERUBIM TAKE FLIGHT

"That's expensive, is it platinum?"

She smiled. "Yes, too bad Mama wasn't here to see it. Why she'd go home?"

"Mad, and even that ring wouldn't be enough to change her mind."

"Well, Gerald bought the ring for me, not for Mama."

"Well, you can tell her that; she's calling as soon as she gets home."

The room was getting quiet, so April went into the TV room to check on the kids. I followed behind. When we saw the Jasmine and Tanya playing quietly, we went back into the living room.

"I want you to help in planning with the wedding."

"I told you I'm not into all that."

"You could help me pick out a champagne."

"Haven't you heard, April?"

"What?"

"I don't drink, at all. Not even at funerals."

"Oh well, at least let Jasmine be the flower girl."

"Okay."

"Would you help me pick out invitations? Look, I have a book filled with pictures of invitations; help me pick one." She opened the book and started turning the pages.

"Wait," I told her, holding the page. There was an invitation with a basket filled with blue, pink, yellow and red flowers. "How about that one?" as I pointed it out.

"No, it's not the right touch, how about something more elegant?"

"Well, you asked me to help. Look, April, why don't you and Mama or Gerald's mother do this? I don't know how to do stuff like this."

"Well, would you give me away?" she asked.

"What?" I was shocked.

"You know, give me away?"

I couldn't believe I had forgotten. All I could manage to say was, "Ah...."

"I wanted to ask you earlier, but I couldn't figure out a way to come right out and say it. Oh, Jeremiah." She began to cry. I held her to try and stop her from crying. Jasmine came into the room asking what was wrong with "Auntie."

I told her "Auntie" would be all right and to go into the other room because "Auntie" and I needed to finish talking.

April managed to stop crying.

"I'm sorry, it's just that Daddy's dead and—."

"Oh," I said, "forget about him."
"I miss Grandma."
"I miss her, too, April. I miss her, too."
After April stopped crying, I told her I'd be leaving the next morning. She went on as if she hadn't even heard me.
"Why don't you all move here?"
"April, I have my work, and school."
"I meant to Boston. You all could live here till you found a place."
"I guess me, you, your new husband, Jasmine and Mama here at the same time."
"Yeah. It would be like old times."
"No."
"Just think about it, Jerry. Jasmine could play—."
"No, maybe Mama, but not me."
"Well, the only reason I asked is that Mama tells me the neighborhood is not the same, all the drugs in the neighborhood. I just, well, if you don't want to leave, it is your home."
"I have Virginia at home."
"Oh well, it's just that I just miss you all so much."
"Well, we can visit more often, then."
"Yeah, that would be good."
I wandered in the living room, pretending to watch the TV although my mind was in Cleveland. I hadn't talk to Virginia since I had been here, and I was suffocating here. April and all her brilliant ideas. I decided to go upstairs to pack our things.
"Where are you going?" she asked.
"Upstairs to pack."
"You didn't answer my question."
"Yes."
"What?"
"I said yes, I'll give you away."
She jumped up and hugged me.
"I'll fix dinner."
"Don't bother, April."
"Why?"
"We can go out or order pizza. You can't cook anyway."
"I can, too. We'll have some hamburgers and some fries for the kids."
"Fine," I answered.

ANGELS ONLY STAND
WHERE CHERUBIM TAKE FLIGHT

"I did learn something watching Mama and Grandma in the kitchen all those years."

I went to pack our things. By the smell of things from downstairs, everything would be all right. Gerald might not be sorry after all. I packed everything, even my shaving kit, thinking I could get away with not shaving in the morning. It would be enough trying to get the girls together in the morning anyhow.

After dinner, I bathed the girls and got them ready for bed. When they settled in, I went downstairs to talk to April who was on the phone with Mama. I was tired, so I motioned to April I was going to bed.

Chapter 16

The trip home was lonely, since Mama wasn't there. I missed her usual chatter about the neighborhood, or April, or some other gossip she had heard from the people at church, or the lady down the street. I looked in the rear view mirror and noticed that the girls had fallen asleep. Each one had a Barbie doll clutched in one hand, their heads turned in opposite positions, lying on the windows with their mouths hanging slightly open. I turned on the music and after one more stop, we made it back home.

I gently woke the girls after we arrived home and brought them in the house along with the luggage. When I entered the house, Mama of course was in the kitchen on the phone. After I placed my luggage in my room, I turned to stare at the picture Mama had given me in prison of Jasmine. I remembered with pride how I taped the picture to the wall by my bed, barrettes in her hair, smiling, with her tiny fingers. Beautiful, she was my little girl.

"Well, there's my girls. How was your trip?"

"Grandma, I'm going to be a flower girl."

"Oh yeah, who says?"

"Daddy."

"I'm going to keep Tanya here overnight; it's too late to take her home, so I'll take her home in the morning."

"Okay. I'm going over Virginia's house. You'll be all right with the girls?"

"I guess so. How long are you going to be gone?"

"A couple of hours. I'll be back tonight."

It was ten o'clock when I pulled into the driveway. The lights were still on. I hadn't seen her in a week. I rang the doorbell.

"Hey, you're back." She hugged me.

"Yeah, I hope you don't mind."

"No, actually I tried calling, your line was busy."

"Mama and April."

"Oh, come on in."

I came in the house, the scent of furniture polish lingered in the air. I noticed the can and dusting rag still sitting on the table. I sank down in the leather furniture as I sat. There was music playing on her stereo.

"Would you like some ginger ale and a sandwich?"

"Yeah, make it two sandwiches." I looked around the living room, not too much had changed since I had been gone. Kyle was probably asleep. I almost fell asleep I was so comfortable. She came back with the sandwiches and ginger ale and sat down next to me. I thanked her for the meal. I thought to myself how lucky I was to have her in my life.

"My sister's getting married. I tried to call but it was late and you had probably went to bed."

"When's the wedding?"

"In April, of course."

"Kyle's been asleep since eight o'clock. I was cleaning."

"I see," I said as I looked around. "The place looks nice."

I looked at her. A sad look replaced the smile on her face.

"What's wrong?"

"It's Kevin's girlfriend, she's been calling here, calling me all sorts of names."

"Oh really, why?"

"They're angry. I haven't received child support money in three months."

"Why didn't you tell me?" I asked as I wiped the tears that rolled down her cheeks.

"You can get your number changed and just don't give it out."

"Kyle, though. He's telling the courts that Kyle isn't his."

"Well he is his, isn't he?"

"No, and he knows that. When we were engaged to be married, he promised he would take care of Kyle when he was born, because his real father died."

"Oh?" I said because this was my first time hearing this.

"That's when I caught him with Tress. I might lose my apartment." Then she began to cry.

"Look, don't worry. Thankfully I still have a job. I'll help pay some bills. I don't have to pay completely for college."

"Look," I repeated, "don't worry." I held her chin up and kissed her. "I'll help out at least till you get things in order." She smiled and nodded.

"My sister is getting married in four months. I want you to start looking for a dress to wear. Don't look at the price tag. I'll buy it for you. I'll take care of you. Okay?"

She smiled and nodded. "I got to go," I said. "I'll call you later, we can talk."

I kissed her again and left. She watched me as I went down the front steps. It was 2:00 a.m. when I arrived home. The lights were off and everyone seemed to be asleep. I went upstairs and lay across my bed. *You must be crazy*, I thought, to tell her all that stuff. What was I getting myself into? I was promising her the same thing that Kevin promised. What if she didn't trust me? I could understand, but I couldn't pull away. I liked her too much. I was angry I never knew Kyle wasn't Kevin's son. I wondered what other secrets lay waiting for me to discover. Their plans had fallen apart, now it was my turn. I wasn't cheating on her, though, that was the difference. Although that is not always why couples break up. Well, I thought, if push came to shove, I'd marry her and that's what I decided to do.

I began to give her money and help pay the bills. I took up the slack while the child support checks weren't coming in. One day we talked.

"Maybe you could tell Kyle his real father died."

"Maybe you could tell Jasmine she'll never see her mother again." She had a point. From either side, telling children things you know will hurt them is hard.

"Well, I would tell her, maybe when she gets older. Right know her mommy's sick."

"And right now Kevin's Kyle's father."

"Okay, you win, but let's promise each other we will tell our children the truth when they are old enough. Bet?" which was street language for *all right*.

"Okay."

I began to keep late hours. One day I came straight home from work.

"Why don't you just move in with her?"

"Huh?"

"I said, why don't you just move in with her?"

I think for the first time I had realized I was going crazy.

"Look at you, when's the last time you ate? You're neglecting your child."

"Okay, Ma."

I first thought I'd solve the problem by taking Jasmine with me, all that running back and forth. One day I stayed home because I had a sharp pain in my side while coming home from work.

"Mama," I said when she got home, "I don't feel so well."

"Well, why don't you go upstairs and lie down."

"I did and my side hurts really bad." I began to bend down. "I think I need to go to the doctor."

And go to the doctor I did. My mother called the ambulance and they came and took me to St. Luke's Hospital. The doctor pressed on my side; before he could say anything, I groaned.

"That hurts," I told him.

"You need your appendix taken out. I believe it has ruptured."

So they took some more blood from me and I was headed for the operating room.

The doctor explained to me what they were going to do, and told me that they would give me anesthesia.

After the surgery was over, I woke up to the nurse's voice. "Mr. Washington, would you like to take your medication?"

"What I would like is to imitate Rip Van Winkle and sleep for the next couple hundred years."

"Very funny, Mr. Washington, the doctor will be in to see you in a moment." I sat up with my feet dangling off the side of the bed, thinking to myself, *How did I manage to get in here?* She handed me a small paper cup with two yellow pills and one tiny white one.

"What is this?" I asked.

"For pain," she answered.

"Thanks." I put the pills in my mouth and coaxed them down with a cup of orange juice the nurse had given me.

"Your breakfast is here."

Ah, breakfast, I thought. The dietary aide handed me my tray. Next to me, there was a young man sitting up eating sausage, french toast with syrup, hash browns and eggs. I lifted the cover to my plate, a piece of bacon, eggs that looked powdered, and a two slices of toast centered my plate; a small cup of orange juice, milk and coffee sat off to the side. I took a deep breath, because I was going to go hungry today. I looked at the young man's plate across from me with envy.

"You have to fill out your menu. Just put what you want and how many next to it," he said.

"Thanks, man."

"My name is Greg."

"I'm Jeremiah, but call me Jerry."

"Okay, Jerry." I took my juice and drank it almost in one swallow. I was just turning on the T.V. as the doctors came in the room.

"Mr. Washington."

"Hi."

"I'm Dr. Steward. Do you know why you are here?"

"I think my appendix ruptured."

"Yes, that is true. How do you feel?"

"I feel a little sore on my left side."

"We'll see how you feel in the next couple days."

After the doctor left my room, I slept a little, and after I woke up for lunch, I called Virginia at work. I told her I was in the hospital and I asked her would she come visit me.

It was six o'clock when Virginia came, she had a shopping bag with her.

"Hi, baby," I said smiling.

"Hi," she was smiling, "I brought you some snacks." I sat and watched as she opened the bag. I looked in it. There must have been thirty sandwiches and an assorted box of chips in there. "Your favorite, tuna and chicken salad sandwiches. Where's the nurse? I'll tell her to put them up for you."

"How did you find the time to make all this?"

"Your mother did it; I just went to pick them up. Oh, she says hi."

"All right," I answered. "I'll get the nurse." I pressed the button for the nurse. When she came in, Virginia handed her the bag of snacks.

"Uh," I said, "Mrs. Donnelly, my girlfriend brought me some snacks. Could you put them up for me?"

"Yes, Mr. Washington." She took the bag and left the room.

"Where's Kyle?"

"I couldn't bring him here. He's with your mother."

"Oh really, what all did you and Mama talk about?"

"Nothing, she's quite a nice lady. You're so lucky to have her as your mother; she really thinks a lot about you."

"Well, she must like you a lot," I said. Virginia smiled. "That's a good sign," I added.

"How are you they treating you; good here?"

"No, they wake me up at six o'clock in the morning, I've got a mean nurse who makes me take that medicine, they won't let me sleep. I want to get out of here."

"Yeah, Jeremiah, I'm so sure your nurse is really mean to you. You have to take your medicine anyway."

"I want you as my nurse." I laid my head on her shoulder.

"You are such a baby," she said.

"Just wait till I get out of here."

"What?"

"You'll see." I tapped her lightly on the butt.

"Well, Mr. Washington, I got to be going. I'm tired. I haven't changed from work and I have to make Kyle his dinner."

"Let Mama make it."

"I can't do that."

"Sure you can, I'll call her and ask her to feed Kyle 'cause you're going to be here for a while."

"No I don't want your mother thinking I'm an unfit mother. I'll be back tomorrow."

"Okay." When we got up I took her hands in mine and caressed her fingers. "I'll see you later." I kissed her goodbye. If I didn't know any better, I would have thought I scared her away. I picked up the phone and called home.

"Mama," I said, "Virginia is on her way. Thanks for the sandwiches."

After talking to Mama for a few minutes, I hung up. I was somewhat happier because Virginia would be here tomorrow and Mama said she was coming also. I lay back in my bed and decided to get a little rest and relaxation. It was nine o'clock. The light shone bright in my eyes.

"Where is Mrs. Donnelly?"

"We changed shifts at seven o'clock."

"Oh."

"Here's your medicine, Mr. Washington." She handed me a cup with a white pill in it. "How are you feeling?"

"I'm still a little sore. The medicine helps but it makes me so sleepy."

"Did you make a bowel movement today?"

"No."

"Well, you're going to have to make a bowel movement if you want to get out of her, Mr. Washington."

I chuckled a bit.

"You had a visitor today?"

"Yeah, my girlfriend."

"Okay, Mr. Washington," she said as she crushed my little paper cup, "that's it. Maybe you'll feel better tomorrow."

"Yeah." I turned over in my bed as she turned the light out and left the room.

The next two days were just as bad as being in prison. The door's locked; you're confined to a floor where the only thing you had to look forward to was breakfast, lunch, dinner, and visitors.

I was so glad when Mama came to see me.

"So how are you feeling?" she asked.

"Tired, it's the pain medicine."

"That Virginia is a nice girl."

"You said Denise was a nice girl."

"Yeah, but Virginia seems to really care about you. You don't meet women like that all the time."

"Yeah, she's nice."

"Well I just wanted to let you know, Jasmine is crazy about her, too."

"Yeah she is," I answered.

"Well, if you were to marry her…."

"Mama, I'm not situated to marry her right now."

"Well I'm just saying if you were," and she paused and smiled, "I mean, it would be all right with me."

I never knew my mother even thought of me in that way. I was speechless, she was giving me her blessing in so many words. I just turned to her and she hugged me. That day when she left I felt elated. I was so happy, because if Mama didn't like something, she would not hesitate to express it, and it didn't matter who you were either. I felt guilty remembering April and how all she wanted was Mama's blessing, and how I wasn't even asking her blessing and I received it. It was almost like stealing.

I was able to leave the hospital that week and I was allowed to go home. Jimmy picked me up and drove me home.

"How are you feeling?" he asked.

I didn't want to answer but, "Terrible, I feel really tired."

"Oh, that's just the medication."

"Yeah, I know, I wish I didn't have to take it, but I better follow the doctor's orders. Oh, and I need a couple days off just till I get my bearings."

"Okay, son, but if I don't see you by Thursday, I'm coming and hunting you down."

I laughed and said, "You won't have to hunt me down. I'll be there."

"I don't want to lose a good worker like yourself; you've been a good help for me."

"Well, you've been the father I never had."

"Thank you," he said as he wiped the sweat off of his face with the sleeve of his shirt.

When I got home, the first thing I noticed was my laundry had been done. I came downstairs. I noticed my mother pressing my clothes.

"Ah, you don't have to do that."

"What?"

"That. What you're doing." I took a toothpick and stuck it in my mouth. "That," and pointed to the ironing board.

"Well, I just thought—."

"Mama, I'm not helpless. I can take care of myself." She looked up at me with her hands on her hips. "Okay, you don't have to tell me but once."

Then I snatched the pants off the ironing board and took the basket of clothes that were sitting beside Mama and while holding all my laundry, I said, "Look, Mama, I can take care of myself. I've been doing it." Then I felt guilty, I felt as though I sounded like my father. I could have kicked myself.

"Look, Mama," I said, "I know what you're trying to do. I'll be all right." I put the basket back down and hugged her. She lost her husband, her mother, her daughter and she was afraid of losing me.

"I know, I know." She seemed to be hiding the fact she was crying, wiping the corners of her eyes. She was sniffling. "I'm sorry," she said.

I picked up the basket of clothes. I'd iron them in my usual manner, as I needed them. I carried the basket back to my room and placed it on the floor next to my closet. The rest of the week was the same; she did everything but give me a bath.

I picked up the phone to call Virginia. She answered. "Look," I said, "my mother is driving me crazy."

"What do you mean?"

"She gets up and fixes me breakfast every morning before she goes to work, she does my laundry even after I told her not to, she cleans my room, I can't find anything, and if she touches one more thing of mine I'm a explode."

"Maybe she just wants you to feel comfortable."

"Comfortable? I'm at home, how much more comfortable can you get? I'm going back to work tomorrow. You don't mind if I stop by?"

"Yes, you can stop by."

"Okay."

After we hung up the phone, I realized this wanting to spend more time with Virginia was an escape from my mother. She was smothering me and I needed to breathe.

Chapter 17

It had been a couple weeks that I started back to work. My sister was coming to town to have Mama help her plan the wedding. Gerald and she decided to have the wedding and reception in Cleveland so Mama wouldn't to have to travel. Mama chose the dress, the colors, the cake and she arranged things with Pastor Brown.

When it was time to fit me for the tuxedo, I felt like a pin cushion. It was a gray tux, which I have to admit it looked good on a brother. I could see Mama's eyes shine with delight as she chose the bow tie to go with the outfit. After we left the store, we had a dinner for the bride's and the groom's families.

I think everything was arranged to please Mama. The dinner was held at the Holiday Inn in one of their buffet rooms; the room was filled with guests. I sat at the table with Jasmine, Kyle, and Virginia. Across from us were Gerald's cousins. They had a big family. Mama mostly invited church friends since it was only Mama. Her brother had died at birth and she didn't have any living relatives. Her uncle died when he was struck by lighting; he was taking a bath when the storm hit. His wife, my mother's aunt, my grandmother's sister-in-law, wasn't the same after that and she went to live with her family back in Mississippi where my grandmother and mother are from. Mama met Anthony, my father in Mississippi and moved to Chicago. After my grandfather died, my grandmother moved to Cleveland. The farm Mama was raised on was sold. The story was my grandmother could not afford the upkeep and since Mama was a girl, there was really no one to leave the farm to. She was getting older, so after my grandfather died, Grandma just sold it. Took the money and moved north and bought her house, the same one we live in today.

Mama's group of church friends were gathered together at the buffet table. One of them, Mrs. Howard kept repeating how nice everything was. "Oh, Georgia, everything is so nice, and where did you find the caterer?"

"The hotel catered the dinner."

"And Jeremiah, how have you been doing? We don't see you in church that often."

"I'm still looking for the right one," I told her.

"Well I'm sure Pastor Brown could help you."

"Uh, yes," I answered. I had two plates full of food, one for me and one for Jasmine. I was hungry and all she wanted to do was talk. "I got to get back to my table."

"Okay, Jeremiah, but remember, I want to see you sometime at church with your mother."

"Okay." I went back to my table and sat down. Virginia soon joined me. I place Jasmine's plate in front of her as she sat down when Virginia came back.

"Have you ever seen anything like this?" she asked.

"Yeah."

"Do you mean yeah you have, or yeah you're listening."

"Yeah, I'm listening."

"This food is delicious; they've got at least twelve different pastries and cake over there."

I glanced over to Mama's table. She was there talking to her friends. April talking to Gerald's family. I guess Gerald was the only one eating. This was April's moment, and of course, Mama's. I was hungry and before I could start to eat, Mrs. Ivory came over to our table.

"Oh, Jeremiah, come on over here, and let me get a picture of you and your mama, come on." Smiling, she motioned her hand, signaling for us to come over.

"Bring your girlfriend with you," she added as we were gathering over to where my mother was. She embraced Virginia and I and walked us the rest of the way.

"Come on, Georgia, let me get a picture."

"Okay. Pearl, let me get up." Mama had on her cream-colored lime green dress and hat with a veil on it to match. She stood up and Virginia and I stood.

ANGELS ONLY STAND
WHERE CHERUBIM TAKE FLIGHT

Mama looked so proud with her arms around Virginia and me. Mrs. Ivory took several pictures, explaining to me that she and Mama went way back, when April and I were "this high"; she placed her hand to measure up to her knee and laughed.

"I helped your mama get that job at the cleaners," she bragged. "Look at your mama."

I looked and saw what Mrs. Ivory saw; she was happy, smiling, talking with everyone, introducing people to Gerald and his parents. Mrs. Ivory took pictures all evening. I don't even think she ate. Jasmine even managed to get in one or two. I posed for five pictures. After that we returned to our table.

"Mama is sure is happy. I haven't seen her this happy since April went to college." Then I noticed April was eight months pregnant but nobody seem to care. Everyone was talking and laughing as if everything were normal and as if they funneled the rest out. I found it strange with a room full of church people no one mentioned the fact she was eight months pregnant and showing. Maybe they decided to see past it, as if they funneled it out. It was too embarrassing a topic to strike up and ask *so when's the baby due?* Funnel vision. I turned to Virginia and began to eat my food. It was cold, I pushed my plate towards the middle of the table.

"Are you finished eating?" Virginia asked.

"No, my food is cold and doesn't taste good."

"Do you want me to fix you another plate? There's plenty of food up there."

"Yeah, okay." She got up to go to the buffet table, leaving behind a plate covered with tiny chicken bones and a napkin balled up in the center. I watched as she walked over to the table. I knew when Mrs. Goddfrey, another one of Mama's church friends came over to her, she wouldn't be right back. I could see them laughing and talking, Virginia standing there with an empty plate in her hand. I knew she couldn't get away, so I began to get out of my seat. But just as I did, they both began approaching the table. "Jerry, I told Virginia she'll have to give me the number to your hairdresser; her hair is just beautiful."

"Thank you," Virginia answered.

"Right before the dinner, your mama said she didn't have any living relatives. I told her, 'Georgia, now you got your church family and we'll come and celebrate your daughter's wedding.' And we come out her everything is beau-ti-ful." I thought she was leaving from our table, then she pointed and said, "There's Carol." Well I knew who Carol was; that was Jimmy's wife. I saw her walking over towards Mama. I got up.

"I thought you wanted to eat?" Virginia asked. I bent over and said in her ear, "Please wrap it up for me and I'll take it home." I went over to see Carol and to ask why Jimmy didn't come. After she finished talking to Mama, she turned around.

"Hi, Jerry, how are you? Isn't your sister radiant?"

"Yes, she is." I looked at Gerald.

"Jimmy stayed home with the kids. I know you're looking for your buddy."

"Yeah."

"Is that your girlfriend?"

"Yes, you've never met her, have you?"

"No."

"Come on I'll introduce you." I guided Carol over to our table to meet Virginia.

"Virginia, this is Carol, Jimmy's wife."

"Oh, it is so nice to finally meet you," Virginia said.

"Same here, I heard so much about you. Well, Jimmy and Jerry's mother talk about you all the time," Carol answered.

"Hope it was all good."

"Oh, yes indeed, it is all good, you know that." They both broke out laughing.

"Mommy, who's that?" Kyle asked.

"That's a friend of Jerry's."

"Who is he?" Carol asked.

"This is Kyle, Virginia's son."

"Hi, Kyle."

"Hi," Kyle answered. "Are you getting married?" he asked.

"No, Kyle, Jerry's sister is the one getting married. Her name is April," Virginia answered.

"He's very interested in who's getting married right now."

"Oh, you don't have to explain." Carol laughed. "I know how kids can be."

"And Jasmine looks like a princess sitting over there with your mama and all."

"Yeah, she's spoiled and acts just like Grandma."

"Well, Jerry, I'm a go on and have a seat and get something to eat. The food looks good."

ANGELS ONLY STAND
WHERE CHERUBIM TAKE FLIGHT

So Carol went on into the middle of the crowded banquet room. I looked at my plate. It was replaced with a Styrofoam container, with my food inside. "Virginia thanks honey for getting this wrapped for me," and then I kissed her on the cheek. She looked so elegant that evening, and I even watched her sit down after she came from the ladies' room, the way she smoothly slid her legs underneath the table, I knew she had a little class to herself. It was the day before the wedding. After the dinner, people began to leave. Some of Gerald's family went back east.

Gerald's family stopped over that evening before going to the hotel. I was just getting Jasmine into bed. I heard April and Mama downstairs talking with Gerald's parents. Gerald was at his bachelor party that his friends were throwing him. I had turned the invitation down only because I knew there would be a lot of heavy drinking and I would be uncomfortable. I was just going to make an appearance, but even William told me not to put myself in a situation were I would feel uncomfortable. I decided against it and stayed home. I went to bed early so I could get up and prepare for the wedding.

Chapter 18

The day of the wedding came. Mama couldn't have picked a better day. I woke to the sound of the birds chirping and it was as if you could hear the Creator say, "Everything's going to be all right."

I went downstairs, relieved that I heard no bickering and arguing. April and Gerald had finally found a way to seduce Mama by giving her what she wanted. She arranged the whole wedding as if it were her own. They had the best of everything. The wedding was taking place at Mama's church, Christ the King down the street from where we lived. Pastor Brown was performing the marriage ceremony. The invitations had been sent out months in advance. Everything was running smooth and on schedule. When I went into the kitchen, I saw Mama giving April a press and curl. Jasmine was all dressed, looking like a miniature bride herself. She kept asking questions about marriage and dancing around in her dress till Mama said, "Girl, now you see me doing your auntie's hair, will you please sit down and shut up!"

Only then did Jasmine sit. I stood in the doorway. Mama said, "Jerry, don't you have something to do; you're making me nervous just standing there!" She was yelling at everyone, but I just stood and gazed thinking about the time April and I got in our fight here at Grandma's house. She didn't want me following her around, so when she told me I couldn't go to her friend's house with her, telling me to go home, I punched her in the eye. Of course I bloodied her nose a bit and she went into the house crying. My grandmother was angry. *"Jerry you not supposed to hit girls; girls are made of sugar and spice and everything nice."* That's when I started calling her Miss Polly Purebred after the Underdog cartoon. No one, I thought, could be that good.

"Jerry, will you please go do... something?" Mama asked.

I woke up from my dream and stood up straight and said, "Okay. I'll go get dressed."

"Go!" she said.

"I'm going." I went up to my bedroom to get ready for the wedding, putting on my tuxedo. I looked in the mirror and saw how handsome I was. I tried looking at my right profile then my left. "Yeah," I said to myself, smoothing out the suit and straightening the bow tie. I felt I had grown up to be a man and giving my sister away was my rite to passage. It was as if I were going to the wedding a boy and coming back a man. I was flattered that April asked me to give her away since Daddy was dead. By then a whole new set of worries entered my mind. I was responsible for April's happiness. By the time Virginia and I got to the church it was full. Virginia was beautiful. When she dressed up and we went out, she would always show me out. I would really feel insecure, so I minded my P's and Q's whenever we went out. I fidgeted as we stood in the hallway.

"Hey, relax," Virginia said.

"I have a right to be nervous; that's my sister," I answered looking into the chapel.

"You're just overprotective, that's all."

"I know he better treat her right."

"He will and you'll find something else you don't like about him."

"Yeah, well." I couldn't think of anything else to say but *you're right*, which I kept to myself.

"What time is it?" I asked instead.

"Five minutes after 9:00. Don't you have a watch on?"

"I like the time on your watch better."

She gave me a shove with her shoulders. "I'm going to sit down. All you want to do is play games."

I made her mad. I followed her as far as the doorway and watched as she went to sit down, then I went back into the hallway, waiting for April to come out and for the ceremony to begin.

It was 9:30 when April came out of the dressing room and down the hallway with Mama. I then took her hand and the procession started. We were the last to come down the aisle April stopped a minute.

"You okay?" I asked.

"Yes, I'm all right," she answered holding her stomach.

When we approached the front of the chapel, there was her husband-to-be, Gerald.

"Who gives this woman away?"

"I do," I answered.

I gave April to Gerald. They now faced the pastor. I left from the front of the church and sat in the front pew next to Virginia. I waved at Jasmine who behaved like an angel. I watched April as the ceremony proceeded.

"April doesn't look so good," I whispered to Virginia.

"She's nervous, that's all."

Suddenly she bent over. The whole congregation oohed and aahed. I heard Pastor Brown ask her if she were all right. "I'm fine."

Five minutes into the ceremony, she went down again. Something was wrong. Gerald was tending to her as Mama and Gerald's parents surrounded her.

"I think I'm having the baby," April cried as they tried to pull her to her feet. Pastor Brown asked should he finish.

Mama answered, "You see her condition."

So they did their best to hurry the wedding along.

"May we have the ring, please?"

"Gerald, repeat after me.

"With this ring, I thee wed."

She went down again. "Mama, help me," she cried. They tried to pull her to her feet. "I can't stand up." At that moment, water was coming down on the floor, out from under April's dress.

"Oh my goodness," Virginia said. "Her water has broken. She's going to have the baby right here in the chapel!"

The first thing I remember thinking was, *This cannot be happening.*

"Someone call an ambulance," someone yelled.

I saw Jimmy in the hallway. We glanced at each other and then bolted for Pastor Brown's office. I dialed nine-one-one.

"Nine-one-one, what is your emergency?"

"My sister is getting married and she's having a baby in front of everyone."

"Your sister is having a baby."

"Yes, a baby."

"We'll send a ambulance there. You're at 1240 Ninety-third Street?"

"Yes."

"Okay, get her comfortable."

When Jimmy and I went back into the sanctuary, April was on the floor with a pillow under her head and her legs were sprawled in each direction. Gerald's mother who was also a nurse sat watching.

I looked at Mama. "Were they...?"

Mama smiled. "Yeah, they're married, the good Lord saw to that."

Then I heard April scream and I turned around and saw something emerging from between my sister's legs. The next thing I knew, I was waking up from off the floor and a man above me asked me was I okay. I was lost. I looked around and saw Mama and Jimmy and Virginia and Jasmine staring at me as I rose up off the floor. "I must have fainted," I said.

Virginia answered, "You did." She began to laugh a little.

"Daddy, did you see Jesus?" Jasmine asked as I stood up.

"No, baby. Daddy didn't see anyone."

After I came to, I walked up to April while she was still on the gurney. "Let me see the little devil."

She slapped my hand. "My baby is no devil."

I smiled. "If it's anything like you, it will be."

I looked; it was a girl. I had a niece. I backed away as they carried April and the baby off to the hospital. Gerald was going with them; Mama stayed.

"No use letting good food go to waste," Mama said.

Mama turned to Gerald as she placed his hands in hers and said, "You go be with your family, me, your mother, and your daddy will take care of the reception."

Gerald looked over towards his parents. They smiled nodding, indicating their approval.

"Thanks, Ma." He gave my mother a hug and also hugged his parents before he departed.

"Don't worry, everything will be fine. We'll take care of the pictures and everything."

Gerald took his parents' car and headed for the hospital.

Chapter 19

Mama had directed the huge crowd to the basement, and quieted everyone as they began to take their seats. Many people were still talking about the wedding, and the fact that the baby was born almost before the couple were man and wife. I navigated through the crowd and found Virginia sitting with Kyle. Mama and the wedding party were sitting slightly above us on the stage. A word of prayer was offered by Pastor Brown. Then Mama spoke to the guests. "We would like the wedding party to be served first, then after they are served we will have the tables on the left side of the room be served by the tables on the left side, the tables on the right side of the room will be served by the tables on the right side, and the back of the room will be served by the tables in the back." I looked around at the three tables; they were filled with food and each had a giant punch bowl that sat in the middle. I began to rub my hands together because I was so hungry.

"I'll get your plate," Virginia said.

"We have to wait till the wedding party is served," I answered.

"That's what I meant." She leaned back and crossed her arms and looked towards the tables of food.

"What's wrong with you?"

"I'm tired and I really want to go home. Kyle is getting so restless."

I looked over at Kyle who was wriggling in his seat, flying the paper napkin airplane above his plate.

"He's told me four times he's hungry."

"You want to go home? Go, I'll meet you back home when this is over." I leaned over and spoke in her ear. "I'll even bring you a plate."

"Okay. I hope you don't mind. I hope your mother will not get mad."

"No, she'll understand."

"Okay. I'm going home. I'll see you later." She kissed me on the cheek and grabbed Kyle's hand and said, "Okay, mister, put your airplane down and let's go home."

Kyle dropped his paper airplane and said, "'Bye, Jeremiah," and waved at me. I waved back and sighed. I watched as Virginia took Kyle's hand and led him out of the basement to take him home.

The room was crowded with guests. We waited for the wedding party to be served. I was hungry, too, and I suppose most of the people were ready to eat after going through the wedding ceremony, plus the fact that we waited two hours after she had the baby before anyone came downstairs to eat. People rushed to the tables, but didn't fight over places; they were just relieved to get some food in their stomachs. I had stood at the table looking for Jimmy. I saw Carol, but he was not with her. After being served at the buffet table, I sat down and watched Jasmine as the bridesmaid fussed over her, and the way she was eating her food; even at home Jasmine put too much in her mouth. But the bridesmaid was looking after her, so I didn't worry too much. Some people were still getting food. The lady sitting across from me spoke.

"I see your girlfriend went home."

"Yes, her son was getting tired so she took him home."

"I'm Sister Jacklyn Hood. I knew your grandmother when she was livin'. We sang into the choir together."

"So you knew my grandmother?"

"Oh, yes, she was a good woman."

I wondered if she knew I had spent time in jail.

"I hear you're in school now."

"Yes," I answered.

"Well, Jeremiah, everyone at Christ the King is proud of you. If your grandmother were here today, she would be so proud.

"And Brother Atkinson is a good man, too. He sees you like you were his own son and we know that here." I nodded.

"Where is Jimmy?" I asked looking around.

"I think they went to get the speaker phone. They're going to talk to the couple over the phone."

"We're going to talk to them over the phone?" It seemed like a pretty ingenious idea. I ate my food and watched and listened as people talked and laughed everyone seemed to be having a good time. I notice Jimmy and Gerald's father coming from the back of the building carrying a phone and a small table. They stood in the front trying to hook up the phone to an outlet and set it up on a table. Then the guests were quieted a third time. The best man began to speak.

"We are going to call the couple and toast their wedding since they are not here."

Jimmy and Gerald's father were pressing different buttons on the phone until they got it working. They had the couple over the speaker phone and had a microphone near the speaker so everyone could hear April and Gerald speak from the phone.

"Gerald, can you hear us?"

"Yes, we can hear you fine."

"Tell April she should name the baby Spring, because Spring always seems to come early."

Everyone started laughing.

"I'm not going to make a long speech, but I've been through a lot with you, man, and that speaks for itself. I just want to say the best to you and your new family."

People were cheering and clapping, raising their glasses to drink. After I ate I made up my mind that I would leave. I walked up to Mama and told her I was going.

"Where's Virginia?"

"She took Kyle home. He was getting too restless. Can you watch Jasmine for me? I'm going to take this plate to Virginia and leave Jasmine here."

"Oh, okay. Just don't be too late comin' home, I gotta get some rest, too, you know."

I looked at my watch. It was 5:45.

"I'll be home by 9:00, probably before you get home."

"Okay." She hugged me.

I went over to Gerald's parents and said goodbye. I'd see them when I got home.

"You sure you don't want to stay, help take the limousine back?" Gerald's father asked.

"No," I assured him.

"Well, at least get a piece of cake for you and Ginny." That's what Gerald's mother called Virginia.

"I will," I said.

"Now go over to the table because they've already begun to cut it up and get a couple of slices."

"Okay." She kissed me on the cheek.

"I'll see you later, Jeremiah."

Gerald's father shook my hand. I had also gone over to say goodbye to Jimmy and his wife.

"Hi, Carol. Hey, Jimmy."

"Hey, hey, what's up, my brother?" Jimmy wiped his hand on the napkin and then shook my hand.

"Well now, how does it feel? You've became a brother-in-law and an uncle in one day."

"Yeah," I smiled, "it feels all right, I guess."

"Anything I should know?"

"No, except I'm taking off. I'm going to meet Virginia at home."

"Oh."

"Yeah, listen I'll see you tomorrow. It was nice seeing you, Carol. Bye."

"Goodbye, Jeremiah," Carol answered.

I went to fix Virginia a plate as I had promised her and got two slices of cake. I carried the cake and two plates in one hand, being careful not to spill them as I walked outside.

When I got outside, I looked for my car and for the attendant that was supposed to be outside watching the cars. He wasn't there. I had to turn around and go back outside with the plates still in my hands to find him. This was going to further delay my leaving.

I went back into the crowded basement. People were walking around and talking. I had to look around the room for the attendant. I felt a tap on the shoulder.

"Hey, young man." It was Pastor Brown.

"Hi, have you seen the parking attendant?"

"He's getting some food."

"Oh."

"How have things been going? Your mother tells me that you're doing well in school."

"Yeah, I made the dean's list."

"Maybe you and your lady friend will be planning something like this."

"Yeah it's possible," I answered. I was getting impatient because I really wanted to go.

ANGELS ONLY STAND
WHERE CHERUBIM TAKE FLIGHT

"Yes, I remember when you and your sister were this high." He took his hand and placed to his knee. "I'd tell your grandmother, 'That grandson of yours is going to be all right. He'll become one of God's saints one day,' that's what I told her." He took a sip of his punch. "Yes, I know your grandmother loved both of you, but she had her eye out for you especially."

"Thanks for telling me that."

"Oh yes, it's time, Jeremiah."

"For what?"

"To come to Jesus."

"Well, I'm still searching."

"For what?"

"Just the right time, the right church, that's all."

"Well, son, don't wait too late, lest the wrath of God be upon you," he said patting me on the shoulder. "You have a good evening. I'll tell your mama we had this talk."

I thanked the pastor for sharing that message with me, and went on to look for the parking attendant.

I looked over the heads of the guests in the basement and a spotted a man at a punch bowl that looked like he might not be a guest. I walked towards the punch bowl where he was standing. "Uh, are you the parking attendant?" I asked.

"Yes, are you ready to go?"

"Yes."

"Okay." He set his cup down and signaled for me to follow him, which I did of course, right out into the parking lot. "Which car is yours?" he asked.

I pointed to the Ninety-eight that was blocked in by the Cadillac. He walked over and began to move the cars until my car was free to leave the parking lot.

I got into the car and drove away. I was deliberating whether to go see April or to go on to Virginia's house as I had planned. I got to Kinsman and kept straight; Virginia won. I was going to see her first, at least. I figured April needed to rest anyway. I'd see her tomorrow, seeing as though they wouldn't be going on their honeymoon. What type of honeymoon would that be with a screaming baby? They might as well save some money and stay with Mama and me, but that might not be the best thing either, knowing Mama. I giggled to myself because of the look on April's face when her water broke. I wished I had a picture. That would have been great; I would have had something to tease her about for the rest of her life.

When I reached Virginia's house, I pulled into the driveway all the way to the back of the house, balancing the plates in my hand, and went to ring the buzzer. When I went to visit Virginia, she seemed to be in a bad mood. I couldn't place my finger on why she was so angry.

"Here, madam, at your service." I handed her the plate of food. "Oh, don't forget, madam." I handed her the plate with the piece of cake. She took the plates and set them on the kitchen table.

"What's wrong?" I asked.

"Nothing."

"Aren't you going to eat the food I brought, seeing all the trouble I went through to get it, senorita?"

"I'm not hungry."

"What's wrong, baby?" I tugged at her lip.

"Nothing's wrong. I've been busy with Kyle all day and I'm tired."

"Oh," I nodded because I still didn't believe it. "Well, since you say it's nothing, then I'll get ready to leave. I got to go to work tomorrow so I will call you when I get off."

"Okay." She kissed me and I left.

I went straight home and turned on the TV. There was the newscaster telling April's story on the ten o'clock news. I yelled for my mother. "Mama, April's on the news." I called April.

"You're on the news," I said when she answered the phone. "The newscaster is at the hospital."

"I know that, dummy."

"Okay, ignoramus, why didn't you tell anyone you'd be on it?" I replied.

"Will you two stop it," Mama said, "so I can hear?"

"Okay, Mama."

"I didn't want to make a big deal out of it," she answered.

"You should have seen yourself," I chuckled, "when your water broke."

"That was not funny."

"Yes it was," I said.

"What about you passing out when the baby came out?" April replied, still laughing.

"Yeah, well, I've never seen a baby come out of a woman before."

"Gerald's going home tomorrow, Jerry," she said. "I'm going to stay with you and Mama until the baby is ready to come home."

"I don't know where you gonna sleep. Oh, I know, maybe Mama will let you sleep on the floor in the living room." I laughed. "No, April, you can have my bed, I'll sleep on the couch." So we agreed that April could have my room while she was here. I'd go to pick her up the day she got out of the hospital.

The good thing was I only slept on the couch for about a month. While she was here, we played scrabble at night or went out on the porch and talked about when we were younger. I talked about prison and what happened the day I was arrested.

"Why didn't you tell someone, Jerry?"

"It was me against them, and *them* were the police. I didn't have a chance. I was set up."

I could hear Mama in her room crying the day April left with the baby. Gerald came and they drove back together. I felt bad for Mama. I could hear her sniffles and I thought I heard her talking to Grandma. I missed April, too, but I was glad I had my bed to sleep on.

Chapter 20

A month hadn't gone by since April's wedding. I was able to set some money aside from what I usually saved to surprise Virginia by asking her to take two weeks off and we would go to Disney World, just me, her, and the kids. With the house paid for, we didn't have to pay rent. Mama and I split most of the bills, so most of my money went to feeding and clothing Jasmine. And as for myself, I wasn't up on the latest fashions, so I was able to save every extra penny that I could.

It was Saturday. It would take about five days to drive down to Florida, stopping to see all the sights on the way down. Her son Kyle was energetic and I soon learned how hard it was making a three-day drive with a toddler and a six-year-old in the back seat, stopping a lot to go to the restroom, buying buckets of chicken and biscuits as we drove. Virginia would take my place driving every ten hours or so. We reached the decision instead of stopping to see the sights along the way, we'd go straight through, stopping only at motels along the way. It was already hard enough and we both felt the longer the trip the more stress it would be on the children. To help calm down the moody behavior of the kids, I got the ingenious idea I would buy them candy to eat. I stated it was cheaper and argued rather than wasting chicken that nobody would eat. Virginia disagreed with me, but I stopped at the gas station, and left the car to purchase some candy. For a while I was happy, because it kept the children quiet. but to my surprise, after driving awhile, it began to make them even more hyper and then they began to complain of belly aches. Virginia gave me that I-told-you-so look.

"What?" I said. I knew what. I finally admitted to Virginia she was right in the first place. So I abandoned the candy idea. Finally, while we drove on the freeway, we decided to sing songs that the kids liked from Sesame Street.

Jasmine would yell from the back seat, "Daddy, let's sing that song again."

I also had the tedious, but joyful job of reporting to the children every few miles how long it would take us to get to Disney World. They were anxious about meeting Mickey Mouse. I sat and listened while Kyle and Jasmine both created their own separate fantasies about Mickey Mouse, how they would meet him and where he actually lived. We stayed at one of the local hotels there in Orlando, Florida. They had a special if you were visiting the theme park. I think all the hotels in the area had specials since they were competing for business dollars. The Marriott had the best bargain going, if you showed your tickets to the park, the kids stayed and ate for free. We got two rooms that were attached. I let Virginia stay with the kids, I slept by myself. It was a nice arrangement since one room was free.

The first day we went to the park, Kyle and Jasmine got their wish, they saw Mickey Mouse. I don't think they were at all prepared to see him because when he touched Jasmine's arm to say hello, she cried. Kyle, after seeing Jasmine cry, began to cry also, so the joyful occasion of meeting Mickey Mouse we all dreamt of was replaced by two screaming children holding onto their cotton candy with drool hitting the ground as they cried. Virginia and I were isolated, left standing trying to wipe the drool off the chins of the howling children with napkins, hiding our embarrassment with a smile, saying to them, "I thought you wanted to see Mickey Mouse?" After that event took place, another one happened, but it wasn't the kids, it was me.

It happened when I saw Virginia taking the kids from the snow cone booth. We had one more day to spend at the park and I was falling in love with Virginia and the children all together. She was so good with Jasmine and Kyle, talk about your ready-made family, except I wanted this one. All I could do on the rest of the trip was fantasize about the future I was going to have with Virginia, thinking she was definitely the one. I saw a beam of radiant light shining in her face and I knew. That's a funny feeling. She spent the rest of the trip repeating one thing after another, because I was so distracted. I was ready to go. I couldn't wait till we packed our bags to go home, so I could spend time fulfilling this illustrious dream I had about me and her.

ANGELS ONLY STAND
WHERE CHERUBIM TAKE FLIGHT

That year I had finished at the community college here in Cleveland and enrolled into a four-year university, Cleveland State. I would take classes for a degree in social work. I'd start off taking a sociology and math course at night. It met three times a week. The math was difficult. I lived in the tutor's office and spent fifty dollars a month in phone bills seeking my sister's advise about homework assignments for about the first year and a half of my college years, but it paid off. I was reading at a college level, which I would share the news of my success with Virginia and Jimmy. Jimmy would always tell me, "I always knew you could do it."

It had been a long time since I had heard from Denise, or her parents seemed to have distanced themselves from Jasmine and me. My mother would tell me how strange-acting they were. Now it was Mama and I that would stay up late and talk about a lot of things, like my father, which I had always felt was a taboo subject. But somehow I think it was like therapy for both of us. One day Mama told me how she and Jasmine were at the mall and how Jasmine spotted Denise's parents and was yanking on her pants leg, saying, "Look, Grandma, there goes my auntie," because they insisted she call them *Aunt* and *Uncle* because they said they were too "young" to be called *Grandma* and *Grandpa*, she said. She looked to see what Jasmine was talking about.

"Do you know they looked dead in my face and kept right on walking as if we were never there. They've only came here once since Jasmine lived here and if you ask me, I think that they are ashamed and don't really want to admit she's their grandchild. I fought so hard to reason with them until I threatened to take them to court. They let me keep her, and they sent their daughter down south as to keep it a secret when she had Jasmine. I didn't know anything till she wrote you."

I confessed to Mama that Denise had been writing me for a while and then the letters stopped coming. She said she kind of thought that.

But now Jasmine would mention her mother from time to time. I would always tell her what my mother told me to say to her when she asked about Denise. Her mother was sick and couldn't take care of her, but I always thought one day I would tell her the truth, but I was afraid. I could never bring myself to it. It was Kyle's birthday and I stopped by before I brought Jasmine to spend some time with Virginia before the party. I brought Kyle's present with me.

I entered the house.

"How you doing, baby?" I kissed her.
"Just getting ready for the party. You staying?"
"No, I just came by to see how you were making out."
"So you're not staying."
"I'll come back after the party."
"You're going to bring Jasmine over?" Her hands were on her hips and her head did this twisty thing; I knew she was upset.
"Yeah," I answered.
"Then why can't you stay?"
"You'll be with the kids."
"So I want you to stay." She came up close to me and wiggled.
"Look, I know what you want. I'm not ready for that right now."
I saw her eyebrows go in and she put one hand on her hips. "Leave," she said as she pointed to the door.
"What?" because I couldn't believe she was telling me to go.
"You heard me, I said get out!"
I started to plea, but I just walked right out the door. I heard the door slam just as my foot hit the hallway. I hurried home and dashed in the house. Jasmine was dressed with her hair done. "Daddy, when are we going to the party?"
"Not now, Jasmine."
I ran to the kitchen phone and dialed Virginia's number.
"Look, I—."
I was interrupted by, "Don't you ever call me again and don't come over either," and then she hung up on me. All I could do was just stand there and look at the phone. I looked up and my mother was in the kitchen.
"What happen to you?" she asked.
I looked at Jasmine.
"Jasmine, go get Granny her glasses on her dresser."
"Okay." Jasmine went out of the kitchen.
"What's wrong?"
"Virginia; she's mad at me. She even kicked me out of her house, and now she won't talk to me."
"What did you do?"
"I don't know," I said lying. "She just got mad."
"Well, Einstein, you'll figure it out," she said walking out of the kitchen.
I already had, the problem was, I figured it out too late.

Chapter 21

A few days passed since I had talked to Virginia. I knew she was mad at me and I truthfully had too much pride to call her. The phone would ring and no one would answer. I thought it was Virginia harassing me. It's funny how easy the devil works when you are sleeping. One day the phone rang and I answered.

"Hi Jeremiah."
"Who is this?"
"It's me, Denise."
"Denise?"
"I heard you were out of prison. I decided to call."
"That's been almost three years ago."
"Well, it took me that long to get up the nerve to call. It was me calling and hanging up; I just couldn't bring myself to answer."
"Oh, so it was you. How have you been?"
"I've been okay. And you?"
"I've been fine."
"How is Jasmine?"
"She's fine. Look, Denise, can I call you back?"
"I want you to come."
"Do what?"
"Come down here and see me."
I thought for a minute. "Okay, when?"
"Soon as possible."

"Address?"

"I'll meet you at the airport. You're not driving, are you?"

"Ah, no I won't be."

"You'd get lost, anyway. How long can you stay?"

"How 'bout a week?"

"That's fine. I've got my own place now."

"Anything I should know before I come down there?"

"Like what?"

"Any jealous boyfriends, old boyfriends, fiancés, husbands?"

"No, I'm alone."

"All right," I said looking at my watch. "You've got to go give me your number." I wrote the numbers down as fast as Denise rattled them off.

"First I just have to have see if I can get some time off. I'll call you tonight."

"Okay. Bye, Jerry."

"See ya." I hung up.

After I hung up the phone, I remained on the edge of my bed for three reasons. One I just realized it was Saturday and I didn't have to work. Secondly I couldn't believe Denise called, and third how was I going to explain this trip to Mama? I could hear Mama say her most famous words, *Boy, have you lost your mind?* I would call Jimmy later to see if could get some time off and call William to ask if he could take Jasmine and I to the airport. I knew at least she was able to see her mother.

I was still in my pajamas when I went into the kitchen where Mama was cooking breakfast. Jasmine sat watching at the table.

"Who was that?" she asked.

"No one," I answered. I was on the defensive.

"No one, first time I heard of no one calling on the phone."

"Mom," I said, "can we talk?"

Mama turned around and looked at Jasmine. "Jasmine, you go on in the living room and play with your toys while me and your father talk."

"Okay." I watched Jasmine as she slid down the chair and wandered into the living room.

"Okay. What is it you have to say, Jeremiah?"

"That was Denise on the phone."

"I don't want to hear any more, Jeremiah."

"Ma, I'm going to see her."

"What about Virginia?"

"She won't talk to me."

"Can you blame her? The first chance you get, you're ready to run off with someone else?"

"Look, it's not what you think," I answered.

"Oh, so have you became God now? Since when do you know what I think?"

"Look—."

"I'm looking and I don't see nothing any different."

"I'm just going to see her, that's all."

"Well, I'll just let the maid know that she can keep Jasmine."

"Ma, I'm taking Jasmine with me." That's when she slammed the kitchen door. The kitchen door has never before been closed as long as I had lived here.

"Boy, have you lost your mind? Or have you forgotten she abandoned your daughter?"

"Well...." I studdered.

"Well, well, there is no well around here, Jeremiah, we live in the city."

"That's not what I meant, Ma, and you know it."

"Oh, so you've gotten grown now; you can talk back to me. I'll tell you one thing... you can go, but that child is staying here; she ain't goin' nowhere."

"Okay, Ma, you've made your point."

"Oh, have I?" she asked as she put her hands on her hips.

"I'll go by myself."

"You better wake up and smell the coffee," she said in a lowered tone. "You don't have any servants around here, mister, and you're not paying me or anyone else to watch or take care of this child while you go runnin' off to see some girl, 'cause I don't consider her a woman at all."

"I didn't say that you were a servant."

"No?" She threw down the dishcloth on the table.

"What are you saying? You're going back down there so you all can be one big happy family? There's something you don't realize." I looked at her as she pointed towards the door. "That's a human being in there, not some toy. So if you think for one minute that if you and Denise get back together that you can be a family, if that's what you've got on your mind, then you can forget it, 'cause you're not going to get her, you hear me? And I don't care how old you get, don't you ever raise your voice to me. You hear?"

"Yes, Mama."

"Now, how long you going to be gone?"

"A week. I have to ask for the time off and I have to pack. I plan on leavin' tomorrow."

"You haven't packed yet?"

"No."

"Hmm, I guess you haven't lost all your common sense, then."

The conversation was over. I opened the kitchen door and walked into the living room. I was hurt and angry; I really wanted to take Jasmine. I proceeded to go up the stairs; that's when Jasmine called me.

"Daddy?"

"Yes?"

"You and Grandma finished talking?"

"Yes."

"Okay." She gathered her toys and placed them in a neat pile on the floor, then she got up and went into the kitchen. I realized then that she was just hungry; didn't think she heard us.

I called Jimmy at first. Of course he wasn't home. I left a message with Carol for him to call me back. Next thing I did was to make arrangements to buy an airplane ticket. The plane was leaving for Houston at 5:00 a.m. That meant I had to leave here about 3:00. I called William as asked if he could take me to the airport. He said yes and asked if I were leaving town for good. I told him the story about Denise and that we were just going to talk.

"Well, you could save a hundred and some odd dollars by using the phone."

I laughed. "Yeah," I said, "I probably could save some money, but I just really wanted to see her."

"Well, Jeremiah, I hope she's worth all the trouble you're going through."

I hung up and for the first time I prayed not a prayer you would pray in church, but a *God, would you show me a sign from heaven* prayer, because I had no idea what I was doing. I didn't feel like going downstairs to face Mama.

Chapter 22

It was funny how my life was taking another turn. I had wanted to talk to Virginia, but I failed. She hung up on me every time I'd say *hi* or *please don't hang up.*

Now that Denise had called, I wondered if we really could be a happy family again just like I wanted when I was in prison. Mama didn't seem to think it was a good idea. How does she know we're planning on getting back together anyway? *Humph*, I said to myself as I straightened all the magazines in my room. I sat all day long toying with the idea that Denise and I would get back together. I wondered would things still be the same? Would I still feel about her the same way I did when we were younger? What about Virginia? I loved her; was it possible to love two people at the same time? It was a wonderful world in my imagination. My curiosity was peaked. I just had to know.

It wasn't till Jimmy called that I came back to myself.

"Hello?" I answered.

"Jerry?"

"Hey, Jimmy."

"What's going on?"

"I need to take some time off."

"Okay. How long are we talking about?"

"A week, a week and two days."

"You all right?"

"Yes," I answered. Then I confessed, "Look, Denise called. I want to go see her."

He hesitated and then said, "Well, I can't stop you from going."

"Look," I said, "if you really need me, I can postpone my trip."

"No," he answered, "that's your child's mother. I'm sure you two have a lot to talk about."

"Yeah, you're right."

"When are you leaving?"

"3:00 a.m. My flight leaves at 5:00."

"Well, Jerry, good luck. I'll be praying for you."

"Thanks, Jimmy. I appreciate it."

"No problem, I see you when you get back."

"Okay, bye." I hung the receiver up I could have jumped from here clear to the moon I was so happy. *Now*, I thought as I looked around the room to get my bags packed, *we could start off where we left off.*

I had stopped daydreaming and began to pack my bags, taking my luggage out of my closet. I laid everything inside in layers; my underwear, shirts, pants, then I took my toiletries and packed them in a separate tote. After I was sure I had everything I needed, I ventured back downstairs. Mama and Jasmine were watching TV while eating roasted peanuts. I could smell the peanuts throughout the living room.

"You get everything together?" she asked.

"Yeah, William's picking me up at 3:00 a.m. My flight leaves at 5:00."

"Daddy, where you going?"

"I'm going to visit an old friend."

"What's his name?"

I don't know why she thought it was a he, but still surprised by her question, I answered, "Oh, uh, Scott."

"You going to take an airplane?"

"Jasmine, be quiet and stay out of grown folks' business," Mama said.

I was glad that Mama had made sure not too much information was revealed. When I felt I was safe I from Jasmine's questions, I headed for the kitchen.

"Don't forget to lock the doors when you leave."

"I won't forget."

I went in to the kitchen to find something to eat. As I searched the cabinets, I heard Mama's voice. "What are you looking for?"

"Some cookies," I hollered back.

"There are none; I haven't gone grocery shopping yet."

"Oh." I closed the cabinet.

"There's some food in the oven."

I looked into the oven and there was a plate of hamburgers. I went for the hamburger buns and took a burger off the plate and slid it in between the bun with some ketchup and headed back upstairs.

"If you want, I can pack you something for your trip."

"Okay." I knew that was her way of making up.

"I'm going to get some rest before I leave."

"All right, everything will be in the fridge."

"Thanks, Mom."

"It's all right, son." I heard the calmness in her voice and I knew it was going to be okay. I continued up the steps to my room.

After I ate the hamburger, I sat on my bed wondering what to do next. I told Neicey I'd call her back. I began searching for her number, which I found still sitting on my night stand underneath the phone, just where I had left it. I picked up the phone and began to dial the number—it was busy. I pressed the receiver down and began to dial again—still busy. I put the phone back on the cradle. I wondered who she could be talking to. I pick the phone up to dial Virginia, but placed the receiver down. *Who am I fooling?* I thought. I still loved Virginia. Maybe I had lost my mind like my mother said. I kept thinking I should try to call her, but I decided to let her call me back. *I'll just act like I don't care. She'll want me back and then I'll just drop Denise. No, I cant do that*, I thought, *that's a dangerous game. I know, I'll just confront her, tell her that it was over between us and whatever we had when we where younger... over. We don't know each other anymore; we were just kids in high school.* I picked up the phone again and dialed.

"Hello?"

"Denise?"

"Hi, Jerry. Oh, I was just thinking of you."

"Yeah, I'm coming tomorrow. My flight leaves at 5:00 a.m."

"Okay. I'll pick you up."

"All right, uh...."

"What's wrong?" she asked.

"You still look the same?"

"Yes."

"I can't really remember what you look like."

"I'll be wearing a red top and blue jeans."

I was silent. "I'll have a sign, okay?"

"Yeah, okay. You want to go to dinner?"
"All right."
"I'm not bringing Jasmine."
"That's all right."
"I could bring a picture of her if you want."
"Yes, okay."
"I'll see you tomorrow."
"Bye."
"Bye."

I just let the phone slide out of my fingers on to the base. *Stupid*, I thought to myself, *"out to dinner," why'd you tell her that? What are you doing?*

It wasn't long before I was at the airport saying goodbye to William.

"Call me if you need anything, okay?"

"Okay." We shook hands and embraced each other.

"I'll see you later."

William walked back down the corridor. I turned and sat down with my ticket in hand, waiting for my plane to come in. I reached in the bag my mother had made for me. *Aah*, I thought, *tuna sandwiches*. There were five of them; tuna sandwiches were my favorite. I took a bite of one, intending to save it for later, but I ate it anyway, just that one. She had also given me a bag of potatoes chips and a couple of cans of strawberry soda.

My mother always preached against airplane food; whenever she heard of someone traveling, she'd always suggest they bring their own food just in case they didn't like what was being served.

I looked at my watch. *It shouldn't be long now*, I thought. I looked and saw a plane pull in where we should board. A few minutes later people were unboarding. I looked around; there was a girl Jasmine's age running around pretending to be an airplane, running and roaring like an engine. I watched her mother pull her to the side; "Didn't I tell you to stop running around? You might hurt yourself."

The announcement came, "Flight 4212 for Houston now boarding on deck 566." Everyone began to get in line, the stewardess taking the tickets as they entered the corridor to the plane. I noticed the little girl again as she stuck her tongue out at me. Her mother turned around and saw her and smacked her on the arm.

"I'm sorry," she said.

"Don't worry about it," I told her. "I know how kids are."

She smiled and turned around. "Listen, young lady, don't you ever let me see you do that again. That is rude, do you understand me?"

"Do you know that man?" the little girl asked.

"No, I do not."

"Then why did you talk to him? You said you're not supposed to talk to strangers."

The woman never answered the little girl's question, she just simply gave her ticket to the stewardess and then boarded the plane. I gave the stewardess my ticket and boarded also.

As I entered the plane, I searched for a seat. I saw and old gentleman sitting and asked, "Is anyone sitting here?"

"No," he answered, "you can sit here. You want the window?"

"No, this is my first flight and I'm a little nervous."

"I understand. Henry," he said as I sat down extending his hand.

I shook his hand. "Jerry."

"There is a bag there, Jerry."

"For what?"

"Just in case you throw up your lunch," he said grinning.

"Oh yeah?"

I fingered the bag and placed it back into the slot I got it out of. I leaned back in my seat to get comfortable. The girl and her mother were up ahead of me. The woman was having a hard time.

We waited about twenty minutes and then the light went on telling us to put on our seat belts and the stewardess stood and showed us what to do in case of an emergency. They even showed the bag that the older gentleman next to me had been so eager to show me.

We were into the flight about an hour and I had closed my eyes. I felt a tapping on my arm. It was the little girl.

"Yes?" I asked.

"I can't wake up my mommy; can you wake her up?"

I got out of my seat sure that the little girl was just up to her usual mischief. I tapped her mother on the shoulder and she slumped down on in her seat. The color had gone out of her face. I went to get the stewardess and told her of the woman's condition. The stewardess followed me back to the seat where the woman and the littler girl were sitting.

She checked the woman's pulse and then asked me to get back to my seat.

"What's wrong with her?" I asked.

"Sir," she said, "please, I need you to get back to your seat."

She took the little girl and disappeared in the front of the plane with one of the other stewardesses, then it looked like a doctor came out and several of the crew members came out to look at the woman. They were checking her blood pressure and fussing over her.

"What's wrong?" the man next to me asked.

"I think that lady with the little girl is dead."

"What?" he asked.

"Yeah, I looked at her. There was no color in her face at all, just blue lookin'."

"Um, um, um. I guess they lookin' after the little girl," he answered.

"Yeah, they took her up front."

"Funny how she came to you, though."

"Yeah, she stuck her tongue out at me when we were boarding the plane."

He began to chuckle. "Yeah, them kids. Somethin' else, aren't they?"

"Yeah, no doubt about that," I said thinking about Jasmine. The pilot came on and said we were landing in Mississippi for an emergency and we would be boarding another plane.

"That woman done died on this plane," he whispered. "Why else we changing planes?" Then he made a comment, "Well, least she didn't take us all with her."

I looked at him; he grinned back at me. "Look, when you get as old as me, you start to appreciate every moment the Lord gives you. I'm seventy-seven years old. I bet she was only thirty. It's a blessing."

"Yes, I suppose so," I answered. "I had two friends die at the age of sixteen. I'm grateful I didn't go with them."

We unboarded the plane at the airport, and sat for what it seemed like hours. The plane wouldn't leave till 4:00 and it was only 1:00. I called Denise to let her know we were going to be late.

I sat next to Henry the whole time. "Yes, I'm going to see my daughter she just got a job and a house down there."

He was very clean, dressed, a hat, a beige sports coat, a pair of brown slacks with beige shoes with a silver buckle on the side. I asked him where he was from.

"I grew up in North Carolina. That's where my people are from. Yep, the South. I came up here before the Depression. You talk about poor, back then nobody had nothing. People was hungry and my parents, well, my mother left my father 'cause my father, he couldn't get a job, and when he did find work, he gambled up the money. Well... that's another story. But my first wife, she died. The second one, that was the gold digger, she thought she was going to spend every penny I had. I shows her," he laughed. "I shows her. I ain't have nothin'. That's when she left. Met her in a bar. That's the thing about them women in the bar, they like men, gold teeth and a fat wallet, so they can walk around in fur and rings and stuff. They talk that bar language. 'I drink top shelf' or 'give me a double.' You ask them to cook and clean and they look at you like you speakin' a foreign language or somethin'."

Chapter 23

When we arrived in Texas, it was about 5:00 p.m. I walked out into the lobby totally unprepared for what I was about to see. There was a girl standing with a sign that said *Jeremiah*. It was Denise, but she didn't look like the Denise I remembered. She was really skinny, her face was sunken in, her hair was thinning near the sides of her head and it was pulled back into a ponytail. "Hey, Denise," I said. "It's me."

She looked at me and I noticed smiled some of her teeth were missing.

"Jerry!" We hugged for a moment. "Yeah, you look a lot different."

"So do you," I answered.

"Yeah, well...."

"Would you like me to stay at a hotel?"

"Don't be silly, you can stay at my house. It'll be like old times."

Old times, I thought, that's what I was afraid of. Anyway, I continued to talk. "I have to get my luggage."

So we to pick up my luggage and we were on our way. We talked in the car.

"So what have you been doing with yourself?" I asked, wishing I had really stayed at home.

"Same old, same old," she replied.

"I see." I remember Jimmy telling me she was on drugs. I was searching for a way out.

"What about yourself?"

"I've been working, you know, same old thing."

"Yeah, still at the same job?"

"Yeah, I'm still at the same place."

We arrived at a parking lot near an apartment complex. "Well, we are here," Neicey said.

I got out and took my luggage from the back seat. As I stood up, a young girl with a baby approached us.

"See, I told you your mommy wouldn't be gone long."

I looked at the child. He appeared to have been crying. I could see the trail of tears on his cheeks and mucus along his nose.

"This is yours?" I asked.

"Yep. Surprise! His name is Calvin."

"Hi, Calvin." I waved at the tot. He responded by pulling closer to Denise.

"Not too friendly. He's a little shy around strangers. He'll warm up to you."

When we got inside I was a bit impressed with her apartment. The furniture was nice and the whole apartment seemed comfortable.

"Nice apartment."

"Oh, my mother and father help me furnish it."

I nodded.

"Have a seat. I need to change him. I'll be back." Denise took Calvin into the back room.

I sat wondering how I was going to get out of taking her out. Her face, no teeth, she looked terrible.

After a few minutes, she came out of the bedroom with Calvin following closely behind.

"You know, Denise, I'm kind of tired. You mind if we just get a pizza or something?" I stretched my arms and faked a yawn.

"Oh no, yeah, plus it would be hard to get a babysitter anyway. Yeah, I'll order something."

I played peekaboo with Calvin while Denise was on the phone ordering pizza. He began to laugh.

She got off the phone and told me the bill was twelve dollars and ninety-nine cents.

"How old is he?"

"Eleven months."

"Oh, and his father?"

"In prison."

"In jail? Why?"

"He sold drugs and got caught."

ANGELS ONLY STAND
WHERE CHERUBIM TAKE FLIGHT

Why did this sound familiar to me? I thought about Rufus and his uncle. Then the room got so quiet.

"I was hoping me and you could get back together," she said breaking the silence.

"Denise, that was a long time ago. We were both kids, and anyway I have a girlfriend and we're getting married," I said lying.

"You're what?"

"We're getting married."

"You came all they way here to tell me that?"

"It didn't cross my mind to tell you earlier."

"What do you mean it didn't cross your mind? Well, we could still see each other, you know, as lovers." She moved up close against me.

"Nuh-uh, no, I can't," I said pushing her back.

"What about Jasmine?"

"Look, you left Jasmine a long time ago. That is not my fault."

"And you going to have that girl raise my baby?"

"She's not yours anymore, Denise."

"You're crazy if you think I'm going to sit by and let you and some woman I don't even know raise my child. I know this sounds crazy, but, Jerry, I still love you."

"You're right, it does sound crazy." I began to back away.

"I mean, when you get your settlement, we could go away somewhere, just me and you and Jasmine."

"What do you mean, when I get my settlement? Look, I'm done with this conversation." Just then there was a knock on the door. Denise went to answer the door. I stood watching. When she opened the door, a medium height elderly gentlemen was there.

They were talking low, then Denise said with a loud voice, "I said I have company. I'll see you later," and slammed the door. He kept knocking.

"What did he want?"

"He wants to come in."

"Who is he, Denise? You might as well be honest, because ain't nothing happenin' here between me and you."

"He's a friend."

"What type of a friend?"

"Just a friend."

I could hear him shouting outside the door.

"Well, why don't you let your friend in?"

"He's not going to like you here."

"Well, I'll leave and you can have your company."

"No."

"He must be more than a friend, if he's not going to like me here." She looked at the floor. "See, this what I'm talking about, Neicey, you and your man-friends. I already spent time in jail because of one; I'm not going through this again with you. I'm out of here."

I was walking out the door when the elderly gentlemen ran inside the apartment while the door was open.

"Look, girl," he said to her, "you are my girl, no one else's." He looked at me and said, "This is my woman."

"That's fine," I said. "I'm just a friend, anyway, and I was just leaving."

I went out of the door and started to go down the steps of the apartment complex. It finally occurred to me I didn't know where I was going. I could hear Neicey yelling behind me. I stopped.

"Look," she said breathing hard, "at least let us take you to a hotel."

"Okay."

"I told him you were my daughter's father."

"Oh? Where is he?"

"Still at the apartment. Come on, it's okay." She signaled for me to come back to the apartment. I was a little apprehensive because she had lied to me.

I came into her apartment and the gentleman shook my hand. "I'm Eddie," he said. "Eddie Crawford."

"I'm Jeremiah; they call me a Jerry for short."

"Okay."

"Eddie will take you to the hotel. I'm staying here with Calvin."

"Do you have a Holiday Inn here?"

"Yeah, I could probably find you a Holiday Inn."

"All right. Well, Denise, I'll see you later." She handed me my luggage and I followed Eddie out into the parking lot and got into his car. When we both were in the car, I told him, "Look, I didn't want to say anything, but could you just take me back to the airport?"

"You're not going to the hotel?"

"Nope." I thought I have had enough surprises for one day.

"You like her, don't you?"

"No, Eddie, that was a long time ago."

"Well, she's a nice girl, she just needs someone to help her, you know, with the baby and getting off drugs. It's hard trying to do everything alone."

"Yeah, I guess you're right," which is exactly the reason why she probably didn't want Jasmine.

"Well, me and her got plans for the little girl. We gonna put her in private school."

"Oh really?"

"She didn't tell you?"

"Eddie, I don't mean to burst your bubble or anything, but this is the first time I've heard this."

Eddie was still talking. My mind was still on the comment he just made about Jasmine. I looked outside trying to determine what was true and what was just concocted for his benefit.

"How do you like Houston?"

"I haven't been here long enough to say whether I like it or not, but what I've seen of it I guess I like."

"So what do you think?"

"About what?"

"About what I said about Denise and me."

I looked at him. "I didn't catch what you said." I was lying; truth was I wasn't listening to him, and besides, I couldn't imagine Denise with this old guy anyway.

"Denise might be pregnant."

"Oh, I didn't hear you at first."

"Of course, we won't know till tomorrow."

"Oh really?"

"I figure we go ahead and get married."

"That sounds like a plan."

"Holiday Inn right down the street. Get you somethin' to eat, get you some sleep and leave in the morning." I looked at Eddie. He was grinning. I looked down the street. I could see the Holiday Inn sign from where we were.

"All right, I'll go to the Holiday Inn."

Eddie pulled into the parking lot and parked by the front entrance. I got out and he went to the trunk to get my luggage and handed it to me.

"Thanks," I said. I reached in my wallet and pulled out a ten and handed to him. "This is for gas."

"Thanks. Well, we'll be seeing you."

"All right, Eddie, take care. Nice meeting you."

We shook hands and he got back into the car. After he pulled off, I went inside and asked for a room. The clerk gave me a key, room 315. I went on the elevator to the third floor. When I opened the door to my room, I saw it was just what I ask for. I put my luggage on the floor near the closet and lay on the bed. Eddie was right, there was no use going back right away. I'd get a little sleep, something to eat and leave in the morning. I'd catch a cab back to the airport. I turned on the TV and lowered the volume and drifted into a sleep which I wouldn't awake from till about 9:00 at night. I looked at my watch and got off the bed, going into the bathroom. I was tired. I hadn't slept since yesterday afternoon.

    I came out the bathroom and thought about calling Denise. I dialed the number then hung up. It was no use. I decided to just go home, realizing Denise had a problem, that problem was drugs. I sat on the edge of my bed, wondering when this all happened, when I was in jail, or had it started with Rufus since he was a drug dealer? Whatever the case, I was getting out of here and going home. My mother was right, I shouldn't have came down here. What was I expecting anyway, a happy family reunion? I sat on my bed and called the airport to see when I could get the next flight out of Houston. The operator told me I could catch a flight at 12:00 the next day if I ordered my ticket over the phone. After ordering my ticket, I called William. I explained to him that things didn't work out and I was coming home and if he could pick me up from the airport. Of course he said yes, and like he said, he didn't ask any questions. After talking with him, I got into my bed and watched TV.

Chapter 24

I can't tell you when I drifted back to sleep, but I know I awoke to the sound of my watch alarm. It was 7:00 a.m. I called room service and ordered breakfast, then called a cab to pick me up at 10:00 a.m. so I could at least be at the airport at 11:00. I'd get there early so I could eat lunch at the terminal.

It was 6:00 p.m. Sunday evening when I arrived in Cleveland. William was there, more faithful than a cab driver. We talked while on the way to my house. I'm glad I had someone to talk to because I thought I was being too harsh on Denise. But he said something that opened my eyes.

"The girl's probably been on drugs a lot longer than you realize, Jerry. That fight you had with her boyfriend tells it all. It's best you left her alone, let that other fellow deal with it."

"Yeah." I was passively listening again, thinking of Virginia and how I was going to make up with her.

Mama wasn't home when I got in. She was probably at church and Jasmine was probably with her. I looked in the refrigerator to see if there was something to eat. I looked but it was nothing I wanted, so I closed the refrigerator. I decided I would go see Virginia Monday after work and apologize for not being more sensitive to her needs and see if she would take me back.

The next morning I got up and showered and got dressed. I heard Mama downstairs cooking as I was coming downstairs.

"Hey, Mama." I kissed her on the cheek.

"I was surprised to see you home so early."

"Yeah, well, you were right, Mama. I'm going over to see Virginia after work."

She smiled. "Tell her I said hi."

Immediately after work, I went home and changed clothes, then I went to the mall and got some flowers and picked out the ring Virginia always stared at when we went to the mall. I proudly put it all an my Visa card. Next thing was to get her to say yes, so I drove to her house with my heart pounding. When I reached the door, I rang the buzzer and straightened my tie.

I looked up and a man answered. I could hear her in the background. "Honey, who is it?"

I said, "Is Delia here? I think I have the wrong address."

I felt ashamed as the door closed. As I walked back towards the stairs, I could hear him answer, "Wrong address."

I got into my car and drove off mad at myself. "How could you be so stupid?" I said to myself. "Here she is with another man. 'Honey, who is it?' I should have asked him who he was. At least Denise's boyfriend did that." I sat thinking what I could have done, and should have done.

Well, he won that round. I'll call her, that's what I'll do, I thought to myself. I wondered what to do to win her back.

It was 1989 and almost four years since I had been released. This summer pretty much was gone and Jimmy had suffered an aneurysm of the brain and was placed on life support at Mt. Sinai Hospital in a coma. I told the news the next day at work.

"It's a shame that his wife and kids have to suffer," Carl said. "I don't think Jimmy would have wanted this way. If he comes out of it they say he'll be a vegetable, won't be able to do nothing for himself." I nodded as I listened, still trying to stay optimistic. But my mind was a million miles away from the conversation. I wanted to see him after work. It was 12:00. I thought 3:00 o'clock would never come, but eventually it did. We finally finished up the grounds for the day care. When we loaded up the last lawnmower in the trailer that was hitched to the truck, I told Carl I would catch the bus to the hospital instead of going to get my car which was at home.

"I'll see you tomorrow," I said. He nodded and I took off down the street dressed in an old white tee-shirt, grass-stain-covered jeans and work boots. I arrived at the bus stop at the corner of Lee and Harvard and the bus was coming. I was glad I didn't have to wait long. I transferred onto the number 10 and got to Mt Sinai in about an hour. I walked across the street and went in the front entrance to the front desk.

"I'm here to see Jimmy Atkinson, please."

"Just a minute." The receptionist at the desk was an elderly lady with gray hair and glasses. I watched her as she checked her list. I even peered over the desk to see if I could see the list of patients also.

"Room 3404," and then she gave me directions how to get there. I took the elevator as instructed, and punched the third floor. After I got to my designated floor, I got off and made my way down the corridor. I went in unprepared for what I saw. Truthfully, it frightened me seeing Jimmy hooked up to these machines; one was helping him breath. I sat down next to him and looked at the floor. I shook my head as I squeezed his left hand just to see if he felt it; to my dismay he didn't respond. I let out a big sigh and thought about all the times he had been there for me, and the look in his face when we would have our man-to-man talks. I wanted to tell him how much it meant to me and I decided this was too much for me. I got up, looked at him with tears forming in my eyes and I walked out. It didn't take me long to get home. I got to the front door and there was Jasmine. She opened the door.

"Daddy, what took you so long to come home?" It was 6:00 p.m.

"Where is your grandmother?" I asked her.

"Upstairs." I took long strides, skipping steps to get upstairs to Mama's room. I told her what happened to Jimmy and that I went to go see him after work.

"How did he look?" she asked.

"Not good, Mama. He was hooked up to a lot of machines, but I hope he will make it." I told Mama that they rushed him to the hospital this morning when his wife tried to wake him up and he wouldn't. That's when she realized something was wrong.

"Well, I guess I'll call over there and see if there's anything we can do," Mama replied.

I paused for a minute and turned my head out of the door. "I hear Jasmine coming," I told my mother.

"She's probably hungry. I'm going to get her ready for dinner," Mama answered.

"I'll do it," I said.

Jasmine was already making her way at the top of the stairs.

"Can I go outside, Daddy?"

"No, I'm going to fix your dinner." She looked up at me and said, "What we gonna eat?"

"Let's go downstairs and see what Grandma has for us." She followed me downstairs to the kitchen and I took out the pork chops, green beans, and rice out of the refrigerator and heated them up. When I could smell the rice beginning to cook, I turned the fire off and began fixing our plates.

Jasmine asked, "Where is Virginia?"

"At home."

"What about mommy?" I looked at Jasmine. "She's sick, you know that."

"When she going to get better?" Jasmine was a brilliant child and I don't think that that story was going over too well with her.

"Jasmine, your mother might never get well," I answered.

"My teacher said sometimes people get sick and get medicine and then they get better." *This is true*, I thought. I wondered had she been discussing this with her teacher. I hurried fixing her plate, trying to change to subject.

"Here, Jasmine, your food is ready. Go ahead and eat." I put here plate down in front of her and sat down to eat myself. I was relieved because she was quiet. I couldn't tell her the truth right now, so I decided to try to cheer her up.

"Remember when we went to the zoo?"

"Yes."

"Did you like the zoo?"

"Yes."

Good, I thought. "We'll go again, okay?"

She nodded as she took a spoonful of rice and put it in her mouth.

During the course of the week, I went to work and then from there I went to see Jimmy. I didn't spend too much time thinking about Virginia. I went to the hospital one day and Carol, his wife, was there. We talked, mainly about Jimmy. She asked me how we were managing at the job. I told her everything was okay.

She asked me about school and I told her things were going well and I didn't need a tutor quite as much as I used to, and that I was planning on graduating this spring.

"Listen, Jeremiah, if anything should happen to Jimmy, would you be willing to stay on the job? Carl really needs you there."

I told her, "I'd be happy to help out whenever and however I could."

ANGELS ONLY STAND
WHERE CHERUBIM TAKE FLIGHT

It was a Sunday morning and I woke up to the smell of pancakes cooking. I got out of the bed and just sat on the edge, thinking about Jimmy. It seemed like a dream, but it wasn't. I managed to stand, get dressed and head downstairs. Mama and Jasmine were sitting downstairs eating.

"Good morning," I said.

"Good morning," Mama and Jasmine said in unison.

"Carol called," Mama announced. I listened as I grabbed a plate from the cabinet.

"Jeremiah, I need to talk to you." She eyeballed me and looked at Jasmine as a sign for me to wait till she left the room. So I filled my empty plate and sat down.

After Jasmine was finished eating, my mother told her to go into the living room and play with her dolls. After she disappeared out of sight and hearing range, my mother cleared her throat. It seemed as though she wanted to cry.

"They're taking Jimmy off life support."

"Who told you that?"

"Carol told me last night, Jeremiah, she didn't have the heart to tell you yesterday. They want people to be there tomorrow at 10:00 in the morning."

I looked to see where Jasmine was. "Okay, Ma, thanks. I'll been there." I finished my breakfast and went on into the living room to watch TV. Jasmine came up right beside me.

"Daddy?"

"Yes, Jasmine?"

"Is my mother on life support?" I thought, *I have to tell her*. I had rehearsed the conversation in my mind a thousand times but it didn't make it easier.

So I picked her up and took her upstairs, sat her on her bed and looked in her eyes and said, "Jasmine, your mother is not sick. And a long time ago she was sick, but I think she's better now. Your mother wanted a life without me and you, and so that's why your mommy is not coming home."

"Are you going to marry Virginia?"

"I don't know, Jasmine." That's when I realized she didn't seem that upset about it. "Do you like Virginia?" I asked her. She nodded yes. I sighed a sigh of relief, thinking to myself that she took it so well. I couldn't help thinking about how I could have had this conversation a long time ago, but I was too busy wondering if I would say the right thing the right way, or would it hurt her, or affect her in any way. I was relieved when the conversation was finally over.

Mama called Jasmine to get dressed and ready for church and she seemed to be in a pretty good mood. When they left, I called my sponsor William and told him about Jimmy. He asked was I okay. I said yes, and we set a time to go to a meeting and out for coffee later on that day. He'd pick me up at 5:00 p.m. It was only 11:00 in the morning and it was a while before I had to go. The phone rang.

"Hi, baby."

I smiled. "Virginia, how are you doing, honey?"

"I heard they are taking Jimmy off life support tomorrow." Before I could ask how she knew, she said, "Your mother called me and told me."

"Yeah, I'm going to be at the hospital at ten."

"I'll say a prayer for his family."

"Thanks." This was my opportunity. "Listen, how do you feel about having a man who still lives at home with his mother?" Before she answered, I smiled and said, "Maybe you and I can work something out. We could become a family, you, me, Jasmine, and Kyle."

"Are you proposing to me over the telephone?"

"Well, I'm just giving you something to think about. You still have your boyfriend staying with you?"

"What made you think I had someone staying with me?"

"I came over your house."

"So that was you, I wondered if it were you."

"Well?"

"Well, we'll see."

"Can I make a date with you?"

"Tuesday. I'll come pick you up."

"Maybe when this is over we can go on a little vacation somewhere without the kids, just me and you."

"That will be nice. Where do you want to go?"

"Anywhere you want."

"Okay, give me some time to think about it."

"I told Jasmine about her mother."

"You didn't."

"I told her her mother wanted a life without me or her in it."

"How did she take it?"

"She took it quite well, actually. I thought we'd have to put her on medication. Anyway, they are at church and I have the whole house to myself. I'll see you Tuesday, baby."

"Okay, bye," Virginia said softly.

"Bye, baby."

And we hung up. I was happy. I thought, *Finally everything is coming together. I need to get a ring by Tuesday*, since I had taken the first one back.

Time passed by and Mama and Jasmine came home. Jasmine had on a cute pink pleated dress and black patent leather shoes and barrettes that decorated her hair. Mama instructed Jasmine to go upstairs and put on her play clothes. When she was out of sight, Mama slammed the church bulletin on the table.

"You told her, didn't you?"

"Told her what?"

"That her mother didn't want her."

"I told her that her mother wanted a life without me or her."

"Why would you tell a child that?"

"She was asking a lot of questions."

"She's too young to know."

"You can't keep secrets from her like that."

"Well, you could have waited till we could have both talked to her."

I looked at my mother. "What did she say?"

"We're on the way to church and she says, 'Grandma, guess what?' I say, 'What?' 'My mommy isn't sick anymore,' she says. 'She wants to live a life without me and daddy.' I asked her who told her that. She says, 'My daddy.'"

"Was she crying?"

"No, she didn't, but that isn't the point. The point is that, well, I was so shocked. I told her I would talk to her daddy about saying things like that to her."

"She be all right, Mama. I'm leaving at five. You'll watch Jasmine for me?"

"Yes, Jeremiah, I'll watch her."

"Okay, Mama."

Chapter 25

When I woke up the next morning, I got dressed and made my way downstairs and watched cartoons. Mama came down and asked how long I had been up. I told her I had just come downstairs.

"Sleep okay?" she asked.

"Yeah, I slept fine."

Soon Jasmine was off to school and Mama was off to work. I kept checking the time. Finally it was time to head off to the hospital.

I walked to the driveway to my car and got inside. This was going to be rough. I really didn't know what to expect when I got there, but I got up the courage to go over there to the hospital.

When I arrived to the hospital and to Jimmy's room, the room was filled with people Carol stopped me when I came in the door She thanked me for coming and reintroduced me to her family. James who was a couple of years older than me, Renee a year under me, and two of their youngest children, Kim and Darlene. We shook hands, then we all assembled alongside the bed where Jimmy lay. When it was time to take him off the machines, I watched Carol's family as they took their places, huddled around her. She pressed her head into her eldest son's chest, sobbing uncontrollably as she clutched the two youngest children in front of her. I had tears burning in my eyes and I tried to pray for God to intervene just for that moment.

Jimmy died at 11:15 that morning. The funeral was a week later and a lot of people came to pay their last respects. He had touched a lot of lives. I remember walking away from the plot after the funeral was over, thinking his work on this earth was done. Jimmy certainly achieved a lot in his lifetime.

It had been a month after Jimmy had died. I was finishing up at Cleveland State. I also received my social work license and I got a nice job set up in New York.
It was June when I received a call from my lawyer Mr. Neilson.
"Hey, I thought you forgot about me."
"Well, it's taken years for the state to bring this thing to trial. They want to settle out of court, you know, keep it out of the papers. I think you should run with it. They are giving you the $145,000 we asked for, so I have to work out some details. I deduct my fees and you should walk away rich as a king."
"Okay." I always like Mr. Nielson's straightforwardness. "When can I expect the check?"
"Three months. Five tops."
"Look, I have graduated. I've got a job set up for me in New York at a detention center. If I need you, can I look you up?"
"Sure, I'll send you my card."
"All right. Thanks, Mr. Neilson."
"Look, since we might be working together, call me Ben."
"Okay, Ben. I hope to talk to you later, then."
We hung up. I was elated. I had gotten my license already; I was just waiting till June to march. Virginia and I had made plans to get married when we got to New York, so I didn't feel the need to change the date. I called Virginia to tell her the good news.
"I'm getting my settlement."
"Oh great, just in time for the wedding."
"Yep, five months tops."
"Okay, so I thought we could afford a house. Now we'll stay with my sister just until we find one."
"Okay, so when do we leave. Let's leave the week I get my check. I'll make arrangements with my sister and maybe my mom would want to…."
"It's fine if your mom wants to stay with us."
"Okay, great. See ya, pumpkin."
It turned out the check came in three months. I received $125,000. *Lawyer's fees*, I thought. His card was included. I called April and told her we were coming. Virginia got ready.

ANGELS ONLY STAND WHERE CHERUBIM TAKE FLIGHT

The day we left, Mama stood outside. I asked her to come. She just said, "Go on, live your life. Besides, who wants to live with your kids, anyway?" She saw us off. I was about to go to the interstate and then I remembered. I made a turn and went to the cemetery.

"I'll be a minute."

Virginia silently watched as I got out of the car and walked over to the place where Jimmy's body was buried. I cleared my throat.

"Well, I came to say goodbye. Got a job in New York. I'm taking Virginia and the kids to move in with my sister until we find a house. After that we're getting married. You know, I still remember the day you told me religion is in the heart. I didn't quite understand what you meant, but now, now I do. What you told me about you promising God you'd be your brother's keeper, I wanted to tell you that day I had a similar experience. Maybe that's why God put you in my path. You were my North Star. Well… I got to be going. Virginia and the kids are waiting. Oh yeah, I wrote this poem for you."

I took the poem out of my pocket smoothed it out and stuck it in the ground with a straight pin and walked away. I got into the car; the kids were playing. I had Mr. Neilson's number in my pocket. One day I would make a difference. Virginia was saying something about calling her mother when we got to Boston; I wasn't really paying attention. All I remember thinking about that day as I drove off, were the words of the poem left on Jimmy's grave.

Angels Only Stand Where Cherubim Take Flight

Phantom
The dreams,
The friends we forsake
While enduring the pain
And turmoil,
Yet no sound do we make.
Angels only stand
Where cherubim take flight.
Oh, gracious Lord
Cover me!
As we steal
In the darkness of night.

Printed in the United States
63525LVS00006B/202-234